He Pressed A Li[...]
Brow. "You Wi[...]

She ran her fingertips [...]
now."

"I don't want you to think. I want you to feel.... My ring, Natalie."

Whether it was his bone-melting heat sliding against her or the dark-chocolate voice at her ear, in that moment he convinced her. This *was* their house, their new beginning. She *did* feel, and she felt wonderful. So utterly right she was dizzy with the magic of it.

"Yes," she murmured.

Dear Reader,

To err is human, to forgive divine is a noble adage to live by. But have you ever been so badly burned that you were unable to forgive the person responsible? Sometimes forgiving ourselves over enduring regrets can prove even more difficult than forgiving others.

On the surface, Natalie Wilder, my heroine from *The Billionaire's Fake Engagement,* has it all together. She's successful, poised, well-liked and respected. However, beneath the mask Natalie is tormented. Six years ago, she suffered a woman's worst nightmare… the loss of a child…and she blames no one but herself.

Enter Alexander Ramirez: intelligent, masterful and committed to the idea of family. He's a man ready to take the next step…with the right woman. Could his mysterious and beautiful Natalie be the one? After a sizzling start, however, their relationship runs into a massive roadblock, and the blows just keep coming! But the mounting challenges only see Alexander more determined to make Natalie his bride. Until a final secret is divulged—a complication that Alex might be able to forgive but can never forget.

Hope you enjoy Alex and Natalie's story!

Best wishes,

Robyn

ROBYN GRADY

THE BILLIONAIRE'S FAKE ENGAGEMENT

Published by Silhouette Books
America's Publisher of Contemporary Romance

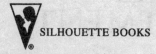

SILHOUETTE BOOKS

ISBN-13: 978-0-373-76968-1

THE BILLIONAIRE'S FAKE ENGAGEMENT

Copyright © 2009 by Robyn Grady

Recycling programs
for this product may
not exist in your area.

Printed in U.S.A.

Books by Robyn Grady

Silhouette Desire

The Magnate's Marriage Demand #1842
For Blackmail...or Pleasure #1860
Baby Bequest #1908
Bedded by Blackmail #1950
The Billionaire's Fake Engagement #1968

ROBYN GRADY

left a fifteen-year career in television production knowing that the time was right to pursue her dream of writing romance. She adores cats, clever movies and spending time with her wonderful husband and their three precious daughters. Living on Australia's glorious Sunshine Coast, her perfect day includes a beach, a book and no laundry when she gets home.

Robyn loves to hear from readers. You can contact her at www.robyngrady.com.

To our Nan, coz, baby, you're the best!

With huge thanks to my editor, Diana Ventimiglia, for her faith and stellar enthusiasm, and my agent, Jennifer Schober, for her brilliant advice and support.

One

"I believe this is our dance."

Achingly aware of the masculine heat at her back, Natalie Wilder bit down on her lip—an attempt to quell her full body quiver. Above the soft strains of music she'd heard his sable-smooth voice, but should she pretend that she hadn't?

Rather than a request, his words had been more a decree, and she wasn't the kind to be pushed. At least she wasn't that kind anymore.

Still, tonight she was intrigued.

On the romantically lit dance floor, she edged away from her current partner's hold—a nice man she'd met five minutes earlier—and turned to gaze into a pair of eyes. Penetrating, entrancing, smiling dark eyes.

Her heart began to race.

Everyone here knew this man. He was of Spanish descent, charming, mysterious—some might even say dangerous. For the last few minutes, she'd secretly watched *him* watching *her* from a shadowed corner of the ballroom. His name was an exotic elixir she craved to taste on her tongue.

Natalie gifted him a smile. "Alexander Ramirez, isn't it?"

Onyx eyes flashed before his beautifully sculpted mouth curved…a mouth that knew how to kiss. How to love.

He lifted her hand to that warm mouth now and murmured, "At your service."

When she'd arrived tonight, she'd taken in a view of the majestic Opera House shells presiding over Sydney's famous harbour. The bridge was a glittering arc to the left of a low-slung full moon, which radiated lazy ribbons of gold over the shifting twilight waters. That extraordinary sight paled in comparison to this man's casual yet compelling gaze.

Be wary, it seemed to say. *Approach at your own risk.*

Ramirez was anything but *nice*.

Acceding to his competition, Natalie's ousted partner thanked her for the dance and Mr. Ramirez gathered her in strong tuxedo-clad arms. Beneath a shower of slow-spinning lights, she took note of his rock-solid heat and masculine scent, so clean and intoxicating the sexual awareness it created was close to drugging.

While his thumb grazed a slow circle between her shoulder blades, Natalie deigned to ask, "Isn't cutting in a little presumptuous?"

He spoke to her lips. "No."

She raised her brows. "Such a simple answer."

"'Twas a simple question."

She tingled at his accent, its sensual slide as subtle as a brush with warm black satin. Reckless, no doubt, but she wanted to feel it again.

"I have another question."

"Be my guest."

"Are you in the habit of undressing women with your eyes from across crowded rooms?"

When his handsome face tipped closer, glossy black hair fell over one side of his brow. "Not until tonight."

She grinned. Smooth didn't come close.

"You didn't stop to think that your examination might've made me uncomfortable."

"Only in a welcomed way."

She laughed softly. "Mr. Ramirez, you're shameless."

"And you're beautiful. So beautiful, in fact, I'm

tempted to whisk you away from here directly to my bed."

A rush of heat flashed through her centre, tightening the tips of her breasts beneath her gown's silver-white bodice. His gaze challenged hers even as it mesmerised and roped her in.

But she wouldn't reward him with any hint of surrender. She was having far too much fun teasing.

Her gaze flicked away. "I hardly think that's appropriate talk, here, in front of—"

"I'm not finished." Hot fingertips ironed down the sensitive curve of her back, stopping at the small of her spine, coaxing her hips that much closer to his. He leaned near, her neck arced back and his parted lips grazed hers. "When you're naked and trembling with want beneath me, I'll devour you, first with my hands, then my mouth…"

She swallowed and trembled inside. "What then?"

"You know *what then*." His calculating eyes crinkled at the corners. "You're looking forward to *what then*."

Her heart galloped on. "Has anyone mentioned you're incredibly arrogant?"

The beast chuckled. "No one would dare."

"*I'd* dare."

"Like you dared to leave my bed at some ungodly hour this morning?" His fingers delved lower, over the arc of her behind, releasing a sensual spill of lava through her veins. "I pulled you back and you stayed another hour. I should have persuaded you to stay two."

Melting from the inside out, she pretended to look over her shoulder. "Your hand's a little low. What will the other guests say?"

His smile eased wider. "Lucky man."

Sighing, she combed her fingers over his impossibly broad shoulder then upward to cup his firm raspy jaw.

Her lover of three glorious months was enjoying their private seduction game as much as she was. Every day they were together, the thrill of seeing each other—*touching* each other—only grew. The knowledge was like a brewing storm…intense, volatile, at times forbiddingly dark, at others supernova bright. But there'd been no talk of a future. Nor would there be.

Some people's pasts couldn't be left behind.

Six years ago, seventeen-year-old Tallie Wilder from Constance Plains accepted that she'd put on weight for a reason. Quaking inside, she'd informed Chris Nagars in the dispatch room of his father's hardware store that she was late. They were pregnant. Her boyfriend had spliced a hand through his shock of dark hair, had pledged his love and had split town the next day. Crushed, Tallie summoned the courage to tell her parents over Sunday roast.

She wanted to keep her baby.

At the head of the table, a dazed Jack Wilder had slowly hooked his thumbs under his braces while Tallie's poor mother had cried softly into her dinner napkin. Constance Plains was an old-fashioned town. Girls who got in trouble weren't forgotten, or forgiven, and at twenty weeks she was beginning to show.

The next month, walking home from the grocery store where she tended till, Tallie had been daydreaming of escaping Constance Plains, of being independent and smart enough to succeed, when she stumbled and hit the pavement hard. A crippling pain gripped her tummy before a rush of warm water emptied in her pants.

Her parents rushed her to the six-bed hospital where she'd given birth prematurely. May Wilder was by her daughter's side the entire time, her near colourless grey eyes glistening with unconditional love and support.

"Of course we'll keep the baby," May had murmured, wiping Tallie's brow as the nurse spirited the weak newborn away. "And she'll be loved in our house. Your dad says so, too."

Her brave baby girl had clung to life for two short hours. Tallie had been stroking her daughter's little hand moments before she'd passed on. Although Minister Roarke's bushy brows had drawn in disapproval at the request, Katie May Wilder had been buried in the Baptist cemetery under the scarlet blooms of a poinciana tree.

The epitaph read, Never Forgotten.

A month later, the town doctor told Tallie that intrauterine scar tissue, resulting from the post-delivery curettage, could cause complications with fertility later on. Tallie didn't care. She only wanted to die, too. If she hadn't been daydreaming impossible dreams, if she'd been paying attention rather than falling and bringing her labour on early...

Four months later, Tallie escaped the small-town glares and thumbed a ride to Sydney.

She visited home the first Monday of every month. Her father had died two years ago from a stroke, but her mother still baked Madeira cakes for church functions, and Tallie's presence still garnered glares. They only made her stronger. She no longer prayed for death. In fact, with each passing year she felt less and less.

Until Alexander.

Now, with the lilting strains of a ballad weaving around them, his chest so warm and the lighting just right, Tallie, or Natalie as she was known in the city, moulded herself against Alexander's tall, muscular length. Resting her cheek against his dinner jacket lapel, she closed her eyes.

There'd be no happily ever after, no family of her own, most definitely not with Alexander Ramirez.

Before they'd made love the first time, Alex had been upfront. He wasn't ready to settle down. However, being the last male descendent of his line, when he did marry, starting a family and siring an heir to continue the Ramirez name would be of paramount importance. The reputation of the woman who fathered his children would be above reproach. Her upbringing must also be suitable, and she would be as dedicated to the idea of family as he was. He would settle only for the best where the mother of his children was concerned.

Natalie wasn't offended. He wasn't implying anything about her. He was simply being candid and, at that turning point in their relationship, she couldn't condemn his honesty. He wanted her to know the score, give her a chance to pull out.

He'd been a little taken aback at how easily she'd agreed to keep their affair "no strings attached" and "for as long as it lasted." After all, she wasn't the Miss Perfect Alex would one day marry. Quite the contrary. She as a high-school dropout with a pitted past and a near empty heart because of it. Still, she could pretend for a short time she was good enough for an exceptional man like Alexander. Tonight she would pretend she was whole.

He murmured against the shell of her ear, "Sorry I was late. I'm close to getting a firm commitment on that medical research venture I told you about.

Dai Zhang dropped in this evening for a final run-through before signing next week."

Alex had mentioned Zhang's name several times. As was the case with the majority of his projects, Alex had been looking for a partner to co-finance trials of a new pharmaceutical. The money involved was staggering, but if the drug proved successful, all would benefit, not least of all dialysis patients. That previous trials of similar drugs had failed was a sticking point with the cautious Chinese business-man. However, it seemed that this evening Alex might have finally convinced Zhang this particular effort would bring about a breakthrough.

"I still could've collected you." Alex's sandpaper jaw grazed her temple before he lightly kissed the spot. "I wanted to."

In truth, Natalie's stomach had knotted when she'd walked into this ballroom unaccompanied tonight. Alex's parents were deceased but she hadn't met his sister and she wasn't certain Teresa Ramirez, the one person Alexander listened to, would approve. Natalie hardly fit the famed Ramirez class. Not that Teresa, or anyone, need worry. Natalie certainly didn't have marriage on her mind.

Finding a smile, she fanned her fingers over the crisp black fabric below his left shoulder. "You were already in the city. It made sense for me to take a taxi in from Manly. I was here alone barely five minutes."

His dark eyes roamed her face, as if he were looking for some nuance or line he'd missed before. "Are you always so understanding?"

She laughed softly. "Always."

Who was she to cast stones?

"When we finish this dance I'll introduce you to Teresa and her fiancé." His coal-black eyes smiled into hers. "They'll love you."

Natalie smothered a sigh. No avoiding introductions, she supposed, even when she preferred to keep their affair private. It would be easier when the time came. No explanations or awkward chance meetings with friends or family later. Just a simple, *Goodbye. It's been nice.*

As he pressed her close, his cheek resting against her crown, Natalie wondered.

Would the decision to dissolve their affair be his choice or hers? As chief beneficiary of the Ramirez multiple millions, as well as a highly successful venture capitalist in his own right, surely Alex would tire of her sooner rather than later. He knew actresses, heiresses, a European countess. She was hardly Alexander's first lover, nor would she be his last.

Or perhaps she would be the one to pull back.

Despite having agreed their time together would be a low-key, light-hearted and finite affair, it seemed the longer they knew each other, the more open Alex became about their relationship and the more inquisitive he grew. She didn't need any more questions asked about her past. Her memories were too intimate to share…too private, and painful, to lay open to anyone, even Alexander.

But for now it was enough to enjoy the illusion.

Tonight she would forgive herself and make believe this fantasy would last.

"Alexander, a gentleman's here to see you."

Alex eased away from his beautiful dance partner to face Paul Brennan, his bodyguard, who stood as tall and broad as an oak. Paul's gaze, as usual, was both shuttered yet cut-throat sharp.

All the long exhaustive day Alex had waited to hold Natalie Wilder in his arms. Who the hell was interrupting him in the middle of a family celebration?

Paul answered his employer's unspoken question. "It's Mr. Davidson."

Alex's brows nudged together. "What's he doing here?"

Anticipating what Alex would say next, Paul rotated back. "I'll ask him to leave."

But Alex's last-minute gesture held him up.

Was it a business concern? Several months ago they'd had dealings and Joe Davidson had come off second-best. Or was this interview personal? Something to do with Joe's daughter? He and Bridget Davidson had dated briefly, but that had ended six months ago. He'd had nothing against Bridget, but if the chemistry wasn't there, why delay the inevitable. She'd agreed.

Alex exhaled and nodded. "I'll come over." Sort it out quickly and get back. His sister had spent months organising this evening, from the buffet and music down to the pink and gold helium balloons bouncing around the moulded ceiling. Alex approved of Teresa's choice in partner, too, which was no surprise. Teresa had her head screwed on right. Zachery Todd came from good stock, enjoyed life and clearly adored his fiancée. Both couldn't wait to have kids.

Alex glanced at the exceptional woman standing beside him.

Engagements…children…

At age thirty, it almost made a man wonder.

Misunderstanding his look, Natalie stepped back. "It's okay. I'll wait here."

Alex laced his fingers through hers. "I vowed that when I made it here tonight I wouldn't leave your side. Come with me. This won't take long."

She arched a teasing brow. "Afraid someone might steal the next dance?"

"You can dance with whomever you please." Grinning, he brushed a kiss against her brow. "As long as it's with me."

A moment later, they stopped before their uninvited guest and Alex extended his hand. His lip curling, Joe Davidson ignored the courtesy.

Inwardly groaning, Alex let his hand drop. "I take it there's some problem?"

Davidson's hard eyes settled on Natalie and his chin kicked up. "You don't want your date hearing this."

Alex's jaw flexed. He was a patient man but he had no time for these kinds of games, particularly tonight.

"We're celebrating my sister's engagement. Please tell me what it is you've come to say. You'll understand I'd like to get back."

Amid the spin of party lights, Davidson's walrus jowls darkened, but he kept his voice low, barely audible above the music. "Bridget's pregnant. She's not doing well. Not too well at all."

Alex's pulse rate spiked. Davidson was aware of Alex's longtime friendship with a leading OB/GYN. Did Davidson hope to secure through him an urgent referral? If the circumstances were dire, why wasn't the baby's father here on the scene? Or wasn't the father on the scene at all?

Alex tried to be tactful. "I didn't realize Bridget was married."

Davidson hissed, "She's not."

Alex's shoulders rolled back. "What does this have to do with me?"

Blood in his eye, Davidson snapped out a curse

and advanced. Paul's large grip on his elbow hauled him back.

Alex held up a hand. "It's all right, Paul. I'll handle this." His gaze drilled Davidson's. "If you're implying the child is mine, it's not possible. Bridget and I were finished some time ago."

"Like six months ago?"

At Joe's response, Alex's heart dropped to his feet.

They'd slept together only once, but he'd used protection. Excepting one, atypical time, he *always* used protection.

His head began to tingle.

Lord above, was it possible?

Two

Party noise filtered back into Alex's conscience as Joe Davidson's arms knotted over his dark polo shirt. "I take it you won't object to a paternity test."

Alex forced the words past the lump of wood stuck in his throat. "I need to speak to Bridget."

"Hoping to pay her off?" Davidson's burning eyes narrowed. "No amount will save you from taking responsibility for this." The corners of his mouth dragged down in distaste. "You and your high-and-mighty family. Everyone knows where your grand-father got his money. Juan Ramirez was nothing better than a mobster."

Alex eased forward, a subtle but one-time-only warning. "I'll forget you said that."

"Bridget kept this to herself," Davidson went on. "Tonight she finally admitted the truth to her mother." His voice cracked on a humourless laugh. "Can you believe it? Her life is ruined and she wants to save you from public scrutiny."

Natalie shouldered past Alex. "Your daughter's life isn't ruined. She'll have a beautiful baby and—"

Alex curled a quietening hand around her arm and tipped his chin at the exit. "It's time you left, Joe."

Paul Brennan edged forward. "I'll escort you out."

"You can't sweep this under the mat," Davidson seethed. "This isn't the old days where families like yours shut people up. My daughter's entitled to compensation." Paul's giant hand on Joe's shoulder steered him toward the door. "You'll hear from my lawyers…"

As the threats faded and Joe was marched to the lifts, Alex linked his arm through Natalie's and turned at the same time the music paused. Below a sky of swaying balloons, curious faces were angled their way, including Teresa's worried gaze, which found his from the far end of the room.

Straightening to his full height, Alex gave an "everything's fine" salute, then led Natalie back to the dance floor.

The music faded back up but Natalie's heels dug in. "How can you think about dancing?"

He studied her eyes, darker than their usual shade of green and yet full of indignant fire. "Nothing can be done tonight."

He could strangle Davidson for making a public display of such a private matter, although it seemed obvious that performance had as much to do with Joe evening a past score. Joe Davidson was a successful hydraulics engineer. When Alex won a government contract for a purifying design four months back, Joe had accused him of "following family tradition" and bribing officials.

In truth, Alex had worked like a dog to assemble the right people with the right knowledge at the right price. That's what he did best. He seized opportunities and made them work.

Her brow pinched, Natalie absently touched one pearl drop earring. "You're right," she murmured. "There's nothing you can do right now. And if the child is yours…?"

Reaching the dance floor, he took her in his arms and began to lead. "I'll cross that bridge if I come to it."

God willing, there'd be no need.

Admittedly he'd had his share of intimate partners, but from the outset of each affair he was honest. He wasn't after long-term. Recently, however, the attraction of short-lived affairs had worn thin. The reason was clear.

Natalie Wilder.

He'd never been smitten before and he couldn't pinpoint why Natalie had taken such a hold of his sensibilities. His rational side said it was absurd, yet it was difficult not to think of her day and night.

She was beautiful, certainly. Intelligent, well-read, dignified. Everything any man could want in a companion. But the attraction—the deep-seated, powerful need—went beyond that. Something in her slumberous emerald-green eyes spoke to him. Something defiant yet almost sad. Something that begged to be released if only he found the right key.

Fact was, whatever unintentional spell she'd cast over him, he wasn't prepared to have their affair end just yet. This misunderstanding with Bridget would be fixed, life would return to normal, and he and Natalie could go back to enjoying each day and each other.

"Alexander, I haven't met your date."

Brought back, he stepped aside then, smiling, dropped a kiss on his sister's cheek. "Teresa, this is Natalie Wilder."

Shaking back her exuberant mane of raven's wing hair, Teresa clasped her hands under her chin. "At last! The mystery woman."

Natalie hesitated. "Alex's spoken of me?"

Teresa took Natalie's hand. "More than once. My brother says you're in real estate."

Alex circled Natalie's waist with his arm. "Agent of the Month, three months running."

Teresa's deep blue eyes flashed. "I'm impressed."

Natalie wasn't the type to brag so Alex blew her horn for her. "Natalie's boss invested a lot teaching her the ropes, sending her to the best seminars, and it's paid off. She's his star agent."

"Good for you!" Teresa exclaimed, genuine excitement shining in her eyes. "Do you plan to have your own agency one day?"

Natalie tilted her head. "As a matter of fact, I do."

Alex's brows jumped. First he'd heard of it. But then they knew so little about each other, or rather he knew so little about her.

Natalie cast an appreciative look around the ballroom, so alive with music, laughter and light. "It's a beautiful party. Is your wedding date set?"

Teresa sighed. "Four torturously long months from now. Zach and I hope to have babies right away," she explained. "Zach's a twin, so two straight off would be wonderful. Having a happy family is so important to us both. Which reminds me…" She addressed her brother. "Alex, I was telling Zach about the Ramirez doubloon—"

Natalie cut in. "I'm sorry. Would you excuse me, please?"

With a polite but wooden smile, Natalie wheeled away and headed for the balcony doors, the folds of her silk gown undulating behind her in weightless silver-white waves.

Teresa cursed herself in their grandparents' tongue. "Alexander, I'm so sorry. I'm not sure what I said but I didn't mean to upset her."

"You didn't upset Natalie. Someone else did."

"Your visitor?"

He squeezed his sister's hand. "Get back to your party. I'll explain later."

He found Natalie standing by the ornate stone balustrade of the ballroom balcony, a harbor breeze lifting sable ribbons off her slender shoulders. Her hands were poised at her breast, her chin raised high as she stared off over the water as though seeing something he couldn't.

In that timeless gown, standing composed in the moonlight, she looked like a goddess. A real-life Venus. Ravishing. Ephemeral. Tonight she was his.

Hands slipping into his pockets, Alex ambled forward. "Wishing on a star?"

She blinked out of her trance and met his gaze, an apologetic smile touching her lips.

"I'm sorry." Dropping her hands, she set them on the railing. "Guess this night's proving to be bigger than I'd expected."

Joining her, he filtered a gaze over her lithe feminine form. Her scent reminded him of morning, like fresh dew on petals moments after dawn. Sunrise was the best time of day, particularly when he woke with Natalie nestled against his chest, her soft, even breathing blending with his.

He brushed a fragrant wave of her hair from her cheek. "I told you Teresa would like you."

"Even after being so rude?"

"She'll understand."

Whether Natalie would come to terms with Joe Davidson's news was another matter. He'd been jolted, too, but he wasn't convinced he was the father of that baby. He needed proof positive and if the child turned out to be his…

Easing his other hand from its pocket, he perused the mysterious moonlit waters.

If the baby was his, of course he'd do what was right. First he'd need to figure out what "right" was. Financial and emotional support, no dispute. But marriage? Were gold bands going too far? Or was tying the knot, giving the child two full-time parents, the least he could do?

Following a talk with his father many years ago, Alex had made a vow: he would marry only after serious evaluation and an intelligent choice had been made. His father emphasised that choosing the right woman to be the mother of your children—choosing the right woman with whom to share your life and your bed—wasn't a decision to be made lightly. Although his father admitted he'd been lucky, the kind of love about which the great poets lamented was rare and therefore not a true consideration; it was better not to love at all than to fall in love with the wrong type. Nonnegotiable, however, was the mutual respect that came from two people sharing the same values, principles and goals.

Alex had taken that conversation to heart. As a consequence, he looked for a certain criteria in his companions. For instance, he didn't date single mothers—too many potential problems with exes for one. And yet tonight Joe Davidson had stated that he might have helped to create one. Talk about irony.

Releasing a breath, he rubbed the back of his neck. "I'll get you a drink." He could do with a stiff one himself.

She caught his sleeve. "This air's calming enough."

"We can leave if you'd rather."

She pretended to scowl. "This is your only sister's engagement party. We're not going anywhere."

Leaning back against the balustrade, he folded his arms, crossed one ankle over the other. "Guess I'll be meeting your clan next." Not that he'd envisaged sipping tea with her folks when they'd begun dating. He was curious, is all. He knew so little about her, which went against his usual rule where women he spent more than a little time with were concerned. Of course, paying her parents a visit would have to wait until after this pregnancy issue was sorted. He'd check with his obstetrician friend, Mateo, tomorrow. This confusion should be cleared up in a week, two at most.

When she kept her eyes on the flickering blankets of cityscape lights, as though she hadn't heard his question, he angled his head. She'd closed up when Teresa had enquired about family, because of Bridget's surprise pregnancy, no doubt. Still… "Do you realise you've never mentioned where you're from?"

"Haven't I?"

With a knuckle, he turned her chin and her wide eyes met his. "No, Natalie," he said pointedly over a grin. "You haven't."

Her return grin included an overly patient look that said he was making a big deal of nothing. "I come from a very small, very ordinary town."

"Called?"

"Called Constance Plains."

"Doesn't sound as if you miss it."

"I don't."

"So you don't plan on leaving Sydney anytime soon?"

"Not unless there's a reason to leave."

He pushed off the balustrade. "I can think of at least one good reason to stay." The full moon's light disappeared behind a cloud at the same time he gathered her close.

There hadn't been a time when she'd denied his affection and tonight her body held no less warmth. Her mesmerising eyes searched his, the message in their jewelled depths unreadable but for one request. She wanted his kiss. Happy to oblige, he lowered his head.

When he covered her sweet mouth with his, the breath seemed to leave her body. Boneless, completely compliant, she dissolved against him as her hands on his chest wove up to hold his working jaw.

Raw desire licked through his veins as his hand on her shoulder hooked her slightly in. When he deepened the kiss, the quiet moan in the back of her throat confirmed that tonight's news couldn't affect how she felt.

She wanted him more than ever.

It had been such a long week. He couldn't wait to get her home, to love her again the way she deserved to be loved.

But first…

Softy, reluctantly, he broke the kiss. Enjoying the heavy thrum of his heartbeat, he murmured, "We should get back."

He was more than happy to celebrate this night with his sister, but frankly, he couldn't wait to get Natalie Wilder back home and in bed.

Three hours later, he and Natalie thanked their hosts and left the thinning party crowd.

Alone together as the hotel lift door closed, Natalie asked, "Why do you have a bodyguard?"

Alex hit the ground floor key knowing he'd explained before, when they'd first begun dating. "Paul was my father's man."

"Was your father afraid for his life?"

She was alluding to Davidson's barb about his grandfather being a mobster. Or was the inference closer to real time?

"You mean, am I afraid for my life?"

"Powerful men tend to have powerful enemies."

The lift doors parted and they moved out into the hotel foyer, which was relatively quiet but for a group of vocal Canadians checking in.

"I'm not concerned about Davidson, if that's what you mean. Besides there's other duties a bright man like Paul can perform."

Outside, a silver Bentley pulled up with Paul at the helm and Natalie grinned. "You mean like chauffeur?"

Placing a guiding hand on her back, Alex ushered Natalie out into an opulent sandstone forecourt, which was fringed by rustling palm trees and the hum of late-night traffic. "Paul wouldn't like anyone else driving the Bentley."

"It's his baby, then?"

He stopped, quizzed her eyes. The B word hadn't been mentioned since Teresa's gaffe earlier. Now he had the biggest feeling Natalie would drive herself crazy with worry over the weekend when nothing could be done.

He waved off the hotel's uniformed doorman then held her dainty hand in his. "I thought we agreed. I'll speak with my people, but until then…"

"You really don't think the child is yours."

His jaw shifted and they began to walk again. He'd assure her as best he could. "I don't. But I'm not so arrogant as to rule it out completely."

That night Bridget had said she was protected. He certainly had been, but he could think of only one form of contraception that was infallible, and it was too late to talk about abstinence now.

They moved farther out into the cool night air at the same time Paul opened the Bentley's back passenger door. Alex thought nothing of the man dressed in a rumpled jacket and jeans approaching. But when the man stopped and reached for something from beneath his jacket, Alex's protective instincts flew into action.

"Can we get a statement, Mr. Ramirez?" the man said, revealing his notepad at the exact moment Alex stepped in front of Natalie and Paul shot forward to seize the man's shoulders. The man stumbled back, the camera case slung over his shoulder swinging as his voice rose. "Is it true you're denying the paternity of a child conceived six months ago?"

Alex served the reporter a withering look as Paul tussled him away.

But the man only raised his notepad higher. "How

does Bridget Davidson feel about you abandoning her for another woman?"

"Paul." Alex hooked an arm. "Let's roll."

With a parting shove, Paul rounded the hood as Alex helped Natalie into the backseat.

But the jerk wasn't giving up. Someone had dropped him a tasty lead. Now he fought for the story like a rat after cheese.

Near the back window, the man dipped his ginger head and peered inside the car. "Are you Natalie Wilder?"

Alex caught the notepad and flung it in the gutter. "No comment."

Perhaps a broken jaw would convince this guy to quit.

Either suicidal or just plain dumb, the reporter slung off another question. "Is it true you plan to marry Ms. Wilder?"

His face hot with temper, he slid into the seat beside Natalie as Paul revved the engine. Before closing the door, Alex gave his unequivocal answer.

"Yes. It's true."

Three

Natalie's mouth dropped open as her heart back-flipped then bounced to her throat.

She'd heard wrong. She *must* have.

Alexander Lucio Ramirez planned to marry her? Absurd!

She pressed herself into the far corner of the Bentley's sumptuous backseat. "What in the world were you thinking?"

Alex yanked on his black bow tie. "Foremost I was thinking how much I despise the media."

Her cheeks burned. "So you throw fuel on their fire?"

Inclining his Hollywood square jaw, he flicked open his collar at the same time he flicked her a glance. "My life is my business."

"Except now you've brought me into it."

"You were already in my life."

"Not posing as your fiancée!"

Exhaling, he pinched the bridge of his aquiline nose and clamped shut his eyes. "This afternoon everything was as it should be. I'd all but wrapped up a deal, was looking forward to tonight. Tomorrow we were spending the day together." His hand dropped heavily onto his lap. "Then Joe Davidson waltzes in and detonates a bomb."

Natalie bristled. Surely he was forgetting something, or more precisely, *someone.* "I wonder how unsettled Bridget Davidson must've felt when the stick turned pink."

He edged over a look. "I don't need to be reminded of my responsibilities should I be the father of that child."

She shivered at the deep, determined timbre of his voice, but she wouldn't let his irritation at the situation—at that reporter—stop her from getting answers.

She tipped toward him. "Why did you tell that man we're getting married?"

He pressed a button and the transparent privacy screen between driver and passengers slid into place. "Maybe I did it for the hell of it."

"Then you need to retract it. In fact—" She swallowed against the clot of nerves jumping high in her chest and forced herself to say the words.

Seemed the time had come.

"I don't think we should continue to see each other right now."

Alex didn't speak. Merely turned his head with great purpose, his eyes sparkling like black diamonds as they flashed in a passing sidewalk light.

She siphoned in a shaky breath.

Clearly this situation called for a break. Maybe temporary. More likely for good. She'd always known it would come to this. Hadn't they both agreed this wasn't forever? Unfortunately goodbyes had come sooner than planned.

She held her trembling hands firmly in her lap. "This is getting way too complicated."

"So you're hopping on the first lifeboat out?"

She recoiled. The sting was as sharp as a physical slap. God help her, she wanted to shake him for turning this around.

"You're acting as though this is *my* fault."

His chin went up. "I only know if you needed my support I'd give it to you."

Would he? Would he really?

Confused—*angry*—she turned from him and glared out the window. "I don't expect anything from anyone."

"I like your independent spirit but that's taking autonomy a little too far."

"Because I'm a woman?" The weaker sex?

"Because that statement makes you sound cold and you're the furthermost thing from an ice queen I know."

She pressed her lips together as regret stung behind her nose.

She was saying goodbye for Alex's own good. Yes, for her sake, too. Two years ago a Sydney specialist had confirmed what the Constance Plains doctor predicted. Although the severity of the condition she'd acquired, Asherman's Syndrome, was mild, he advised she not attempt to fall pregnant. If she happened to conceive, the risks to a foetus were grave and many.

She didn't want to see anyone hurt, including Bridget's unborn babe. She refused to stand in the way. Refused to hang on to silly Cinderella dreams that had zip chance of coming true.

An image of a tiny newborn's hand flashed into her mind, and the light outside smudged as moisture blurred her vision.

Holding her roiling stomach, she concentrated to school her features and summon a level tone. "I would like to be dropped at my apartment, please."

"No, *carino*. We'll spend the night together at my home."

Her fingers strangled her clutch purse. She wanted

to scream at him, tell him she wasn't worth the trouble. She wanted to jump out of this car and run as fast and as far as she could.

Instead she sent a thin smile. "Don't you get it? It's over, Alex. The boat's already sailed."

His dark eyes searched hers before narrowing almost imperceptibly. As the trip-wire tension tightened more, she quivered inside but didn't back down. For everyone's sake, she couldn't.

Finally he sat back against the black leather seat. A muscle in his jaw twitched before he nodded and exhaled. "You're right. Of course you shouldn't be dragged into this. Forgive me."

She gaped at him. Was he purposely trying to guilt her out? He'd said he needed her support. She'd flatly refused and *still* he forgave her.

Her fingers itched to touch his hard thigh. To let him know that she did care, and too much. Instead she clenched her hand into the cool silk of her dress. If Alex was the father of that baby, he didn't need distractions. He would need to focus on priorities. She only wished she could explain.

She wasn't the woman he thought her to be.

Dropping her head, she bit her lip.

"Alex, I—"

He found her gaze then wrapped an arm around her. His cheek pressed against her crown, he tugged her close.

"We're both upset. Too upset to talk. Be still now and let me hold you for a while."

Alex asked Paul to head for her address and when the car pulled up in front of her apartment building five minutes later, he slid out and opened her door.

"I'll tell Paul to come back in the morning," he told her, extending his hand.

She accepted his hand, so warm and big folded around hers, but she couldn't accept the offer, no matter how safe and adored he made her feel. If she could hold on, be strong a moment longer…

"I'd rather say good-night here." She managed a trite smile while her heart—her icy, barren heart—steadied itself not to break. "It's been nice."

Not listening, he cupped her nape, lowered his head to kiss her. But she turned her face and his warm lips grazed her temple.

"Good night, Alexander."

He stepped away, stood stock still. Then, like an unleashed hurricane, he swung back toward the Bentley, his gravelled words trailing behind.

"I'll say good-night, Natalie. But not goodbye."

The next morning, Alex scowled at the page five headline.

Playboy to Marry Outsider. Socialite Girlfriend Pregnant.

Cursing, he hurled the paper at his kitchen counter.

His girl had left him, he'd been publicly hailed as a two-timing bastard and, as a side order, Dai Zhang must be wondering if Alexander Ramirez wasn't a chip off his amoral grandfather's block.

Every one of his ventures was run above reproach. Zhang's money was destined for a sound project, one into which Alex had invested a fair stake of his own capital. He believed these research studies would make a difference, not only to his personal worth but also to the medical community who would benefit from improvements made to vascular tolerance of dialysis-dependent patients.

After reading that headline, however, it would be no surprise if Zhang, a respected businessman known for his high standard of principles, pulled out. Alex had worked hard to convince Zhang that these studies would succeed where others had failed, but this publicity made Alexander Ramirez look like a man who couldn't be trusted. Particularly if this so called engagement was called off the same week it was announced.

He rubbed the back of his neck.

Unfortunately after last night's events, Natalie had pulled the pin on their affair. This morning's headlines would have her back up all the more. But Alex wasn't prepared to have it end there.

The living room extension pealed.

Alex strode over, grabbed the receiver and growled, "Call back."

"Mr. Ramirez?"

Unease rippled up his spine. "Who is this?" The voice sounded familiar. The next second he knew why.

"Mr. Ramirez, when are your nuptials taking place?"

His teeth clenched. "How did you get this number?"

"Natalie Wilder is unavailable for comment," the reporter continued. "Does this mean the engagement's off? Can you confirm that the party last night was a double celebration?"

Imagining the phone was the reporter's head, Alex slammed the receiver down. Throwing up his hands, he strode away.

How to go forward.

What to do to save this mess from disintegrating more.

Then his faculties doubled back and swooped upon a phrase. Natalie was unavailable for comment? That reporter must've put her through the wringer already this morning.

He speed-dialled Natalie's cell phone. Message bank. He got voice mail at her home number. Only one other place she would be.

When Natalie answered her office extension on the second ring, Alex sank into a nearby chair.

He smiled. "Good morning, *carino.*"

"Alex?" Two beats of silence. "I'm at the office."

"We need to talk."

"I'm not talking to anyone today unless they want to buy a property. I—I'm sorry but I have to go."

She disconnected and he hung up, drummed his fingers on the desk and glared at the phone. "Stubborn woman." Which was one of the reasons he liked her so much.

Alex stopped midthought.

What if, rather than a brash invention, his statement to that reporter had merely been a little premature? Now that the claim was out, perhaps he ought to make use of it, and in more ways than one.

Zhang was a man of principle, as was Alex. At the moment, nothing could be done about the paternity accusation. But perhaps he should stand by his engagement announcement. To retract now would only make him appear even less honorable in Zhang's eyes, and when the paternity test came back, his name would be cleared.

And then there was Natalie.

When he married, he wanted a solid union: a calm, safe harbour for his children to grow up and excel in. Natalie seemed to possess all the qualities he admired—independence, charm, intelligence. And he couldn't downplay how good they were together in the bedroom. Surely he could never tire of holding such a warm, giving body close to his. It stood to reason that kind of sexual compatibility would be a significant asset to any marriage.

No doubt Bridget would make some other man extremely happy. Her pedigree as A1 and she was sweet natured as well as attractive. But, even if it was proven that he had indeed fathered her child, Alex couldn't contemplate sharing his life with Bridget Davidson. Natalie, on the other hand, would make a perfect wife. A wonderful mother.

Perhaps it was time.

He pushed up out the chair, entered his study and dialled open the sequenced lock on his desk's drawer safe. A moment later he held the doubloon, a near priceless heirloom handed down from generation to generation. He'd respected its history, had every intention of following tradition. But now, as never before, he understood its true worth. He would do what was needed to carry on its proper succession.

And that meant winning Natalie Wilder back.

Four

Mateo Celeca swung open his harbor-side residence front door and gripped his friend's hand. After a brief brotherly hug, he waved Alex through to the parquet entry.

"There's a lot to be said for success," Mateo closed the heavy door. "Finding time to catch up unfortunately isn't one of them." He folded his arms and slanted his head. "You look well, my friend."

Alex took in Mateo's olive complexion, striking today against his billowy white shirt and calico trousers. "You look better than well."

"It's the Mediterranean sun. When I visit home, I

don't want to return. Then Mama starts with her matchmaking, setting up chance meetings with 'nice girls', and I'm reminded why I need to get back."

Alex joined in Mateo's hearty chuckle. He'd visited "home" with Mateo one summer in their university days. Mama Celeca, Mateo's grandmother, was a small lady with a big heart who believed every good man deserved a good woman. That summer he and Mateo had barely escaped Italy with their bachelorhood intact.

"You'll find your Miss Right one day, Mat."

"Perhaps you can give me some pointers."

Alex cocked a brow. "You've read this morning's paper, then."

His hand resting on his friend's back, Mateo ushered Alex through, past the polished honeywood staircase and down a wide hall, which boasted countless heirlooms and antiques, some dating back many centuries. Alex's three-story Vaucluse residence was outstanding by anyone's standards, but it still fell short of this kind of grandeur.

Mateo strolled with Alex toward the rear of his immaculate home. "From this morning's story, your situation sounds…complicated."

Alex exhaled. "I've heard that before."

"From the expectant mother?"

"From the woman I'm sleeping with."

"I take it you're not happy with the father-to-be situation."

"I could think of better scenarios." Like Natalie being the woman pregnant with his child. That he could handle.

They entered the kitchen, an enormous sparkling affair, made all the more inviting by the faint scent of citrus and freshly grilled bacon.

Mateo retrieved two *demitasses* from an overhead cupboard and set the cups next to the espresso pot. "How are the women in your life coping?"

Alex gripped the back of a Chippendale chair. "One I haven't spoken with in over six months. The other doesn't want to see me again."

Reaching for the pot handle, Mateo paused. "Perhaps I should offer you something stronger."

Alex grinned. "Coffee's good."

Drinks poured, they moved out into the cobblestone courtyard. On the expansive back lawn, giant topiaries were pruned into animal shapes…a lion, a bull, two rams locking horns. A Mediterranean style water feature provided the perfect backdrop.

After setting his cup on the table, Alex lowered into cushioned wrought iron chair and Mateo did the same then asked, "How can I help?"

"I need to find out if I'm the father of that baby, and I need to find out fast."

"Estimated dates?"

"If I am the father, twenty-four weeks." He'd checked his PDA calendar late last night.

"Gestational age would be twenty-six." Mateo's pensive look cleared. "To get a more accurate estimate, we need an ultrasound. Scans are routine. Her GP or OB would likely have scheduled at least one. There's no risk to mother or unborn child." Elbows on the chair arms, he laced his fingers, index fingers steepled. "Now for some good news regarding prenatal paternity tests."

Alex rubbed his brow. He could use all the good news he could get.

"Nowadays they're easy to perform and results are available within days," Mateo told him. "We need a blood sample from the mother and a simple mouth swab from you. The results are one hundred percent accurate on negative identification and ninety-nine point nine percent accurate on positive."

"So if I'm *not* the father of the baby we'll know conclusively."

Mateo nodded and reached for his cup. "If you'd like the lady to see me, I'll happily fit her in and arrange for the tests to be performed."

Sounded good. "I'll speak with Bridget…though I'll need to get past her father first."

"As I recall, you're not Joe Davidson's favourite person."

Mateo knew about the hydraulics contract affair. "After last night I've officially hit the bottom of his Christmas card list."

Mateo sipped, shrugged. "You have better things to worry about."

Alex huffed over a wry grin. "Want to hear the real kick in the pants? Three months ago I met a woman I share an amazing chemistry with and now she wants to end our affair."

"So you love this other woman?"

Alex sat back and gazed at the half-dozen sparrows darting across the flawless blue sky. "No. But I do know I love being with her." Especially in the bedroom.

His parents had been in love. As a child their bond had made him feel safe. As an adult it had made him proud. Teresa and Zach had the right recipe, too. Their till-death-us-do-part vibes radiated out, an invisible yet powerful force. But he didn't see that kind of all-consuming love in his future.

He agreed wholeheartedly with his father's advice about choosing the right woman to marry. Raymond Vacanti, a friend from university days, had been less analytical. The month after Ray was left a sizeable inheritance, he'd fallen hard for a gorgeous, streetwise blonde. Two years into the marriage, Blondie got herself a good lawyer, filed for divorce, was awarded most of Ray's money then moved onto the next chump. Anyone could see that woman was a heartless tramp. Poor Ray, however, had been blinded by love.

Alex had made his mind up early never to leave

himself open like that. As his father had said, better not to love at all than to fall in love with the wrong kind of woman.

But Natalie…

Alex sat up and tugged his ear. "Natalie's special."

Mateo white teeth flashed. "That does sound serious."

"I did say I intended to marry her."

Mateo's gaze dropped to his middle fingertip circling the rim of his cup. "And if you are the father of Bridget Davidson's baby?"

"Guess we'll know soon enough."

"Indeed." Mateo thought for a moment, then downed his coffee and sat forward. "I have tennis booked with Eddie Boxwell at eleven. Care for a hit? I promise to let you win a set."

Alex chuckled. "Such a generous man." He eased to his feet. "I have another stop to make this morning."

"Bridget."

"Natalie." He cringed. "This *is* complicated."

"You can't change the outcome of that child's paternity."

"And I can't turn back time."

Mateo pushed to stand and strolled with Alex back toward the kitchen. "It'll work out."

"Is that your bedside manner talking?"

"Is it helping?"

Alex grinned. "I'll let you know in a few days."

* * *

Fifteen minutes later, after stopping to make a purchase, Alex entered the reception area of Phil McPherson's Real Estate. A number of clients sat with attentive agents among strategically placed desks. In fact, the place was buzzing, but Natalie was nowhere to be seen.

On slick castors, the receptionist rolled a chair over from her workstation to the main desk.

"Can I help you, sir?"

Hands landing on the chest-high counter, Alex craned his neck to peer around the photocopier corner. "I want to buy a property. Nothing under ten million. I need your top agent."

The woman's chocolate-brown eyes rounded before she surreptitiously examined his monogrammed shirt, his Swiss brand watch. Then, doubling up on her smile, she rang through to an extension.

"Natalie, a gentleman here wants to look at properties." A pause. "But he's interested in nothing under ten mill." She stole a glance at him from beneath her lashes. "Uh-huh. I'll let him know." She replaced the receiver and beamed over an anything-you-want smile. "Natalie Wilder will be right out."

Her sentence wasn't finished before Natalie breezed out from a back office, her gait catwalk-model worthy, her soft sable hair pulled back in an elegant workplace twist. When their gazes clashed, she stopped dead and the professional smile slid from her face.

"*You.*"

He could almost smell her fresh flowery scent from here. Could almost feel her sensuous curves moulded against his. God, he'd missed having her share his bed last night. Tonight they'd make up the deficit.

When her eyes narrowed, he remembered his story, which, he decided now, was true. Visiting Mateo this morning made him realise he needed to upgrade. More than that. His sleek and sizeable bachelor pad had served a purpose but now he would invest in a real home. A place in which he envisaged a woman. The sensual, bristling, goddess of a woman standing before him.

He nudged his chin at a poster to the right of the reception station. "I'd like to see that property."

Natalie knotted her arms over her smart navy blue dress. "Sorry, I'm unavailable."

He merely grinned. Wrong answer.

While the receptionist gaped at Natalie, Alex opened his mouth to coax her to agree, but another voice interrupted their discussion.

"Natalie, would you come through to my office, please?"

Alex's attention skated over to a fifty-something-year-old who wore blindingly shiny shoes and slicked back hair. From the glint in his eye, Alex saw he was a man of purpose. The sign on his office door read, Principal, Phil McPherson.

Natalie held her breath.

She'd told Alex last night it was over. She'd told him this morning she wasn't interested in meeting. Yet he'd ignored her—surprise, surprise—and now she had Phil breathing down her neck. If her boss had heard any part of their conversation, she knew what he wanted and it wasn't to collect lunch orders.

Natalie eyed Alex. He looked so in control, so breathtakingly masculine and commanding, in deep blue jeans. The man was hot, pure and simple, in Armani or denim, fully clothed or without a stitch. Then she slid a look over to her boss and his all-seeing eyes.

No use avoiding it.

A moment later, Phil closed his office door and, clasping his hands behind his back, rocked back on his heels. "Is there some problem, Nat?"

She tried for blasé. "No problem, Phil."

"Then I suggest you show that man his property."

"If you don't mind, I'd rather some other agent look after him."

"Sure. If you don't mind finding another job." Phil strode toward his desk. "You, better than most, know the commission on that size sale."

"Of course I know, but—"

"Here's something you obviously don't know."

He held up today's newspaper, folded back to that dreaded page five. She'd almost hyperventilated this morning when she'd flicked through and had seen the photos: a picture of Alex looking devilish handsome at some black-tie romp had been butted up against a studio headshot of a stunning looking Bridget Davidson. It made Natalie wonder what on earth Alex saw in nothing-out-of-the-box her.

Phil dropped the paper. "That man is Alexander Ramirez."

"I can explain—"

"Your personal life and lovers' spats are none of my concern. I do know the phones are running hotter than usual this morning, I'm guessing because the today's headline girl works here. I also know Ramirez is a serious man with serious money." The groove between his thick dark brows eased as he tossed the paper back on his desk, next to his toppling in tray. "You're the best agent I have. We need every commission we can get. These aren't the best of times. We can't afford to pass up even the suggestion of a possible sale."

She chewed her lip.

The market was in a ditch, the more expensive properties included. Last week, a long standing agency had closed its doors. She couldn't tell Phil that Alex's enquiry was a ruse to get her alone. Or perhaps Phil suspected as much but was prepared to go forward with the inspection on the off chance the query ended in a sale.

No matter how she rationalised, when push came to shove, Phil called the shots.

Beaten, she shrugged. "You're the boss."

Phil slipped in behind his desk. "And you're a trooper."

She exited Phil's office, closed the door and lifted her chin. Alex's onyx eyes burned into hers. Oh, yes, he was serious, all right.

She moved to join him, crossing her arms again, a bid to convey some pretence of distance, not that she thought he would sweep her up and whisk her away. At least she didn't think he would.

She cleared her throat. "Just so you know, I have a busy day ahead of me."

His grin was lopsided and inherently sexy.

She swallowed and knotted her arms more securely over her churning stomach. "This won't do any good."

"Are you going to show me this property or not?"

"I'm going to show you this property, then I'm going to get on with my day." When his grin eased wider, she dropped her arms and threw back her shoulders. "I'm not kidding."

He took her elbow. "Neither am I."

Five

Alex insisted on taking his car. He thumbed the vendor's street into the GPS and a short time later pulled the gleaming black sports car into the exclusive address.

Natalie depressed a remote button and, like curtains introducing a spectacular stage, the colossal iron gates fanned open. Tall pencil pines stood guard on either side of a long paved drive, and immaculate gardens greeted them with stunning spring bouquets. At the far end of an emerald lawn resided a magnificent rendered building.

The Quinton mansion.

Parking beneath the enormous front portico, its columns twined with lemon bougainvillea, Alex slid out from the driver's side and swung open her door. Stepping out, she scanned the interior. The air smelled of sweet floral perfume and generations of money.

"The owners are visiting the U.S.," she told him in a professional tone. "They're eager to sell."

She felt his gaze on her, moving over her hair, down her limbs, leaving a glorious blistering heat in its wake.

Brushing down her dress, she willed the telltale fire from her cheeks. They hadn't spoken during the drive here but she'd felt the force of Alex's concentration as he'd negotiated the Sydney streets. He'd been formulating a foolproof plan to get what he wanted.

But she wasn't a fool anymore, even where Alexander was concerned.

"The reporters have been onto you this morning," he said.

She sighed. *So it begins.*

She moved ahead, up the broad stone steps that led to a pristine slate veranda. "The house has six large bedrooms, all with private sitting rooms and imported marble bathrooms—"

"They've been onto me, too."

"—as well as two offices, a home theatre, an indoor pool along with outdoor swimming facilities, including sauna and ten-person hot tub—"

"I have an idea."

She spun on him. "So do I. It entails getting back to my office and diving into some real work."

His dark eyes sparkled in the dappled sunlight. "So you're curious."

The stern look slipped from her face, but damned if she'd grin back. "You're incorrigible."

"I'll take that as a compliment." His arm went out to bring her close but she dodged and headed toward the double front doors.

She turned the lock and stepped into a grand vestibule while Alex's voice came again from behind. "The publicity hype will only get worse."

She'd weather it. After Alex retracted his engagement statement, she'd simply keep her head down. Get on with her life. And never, ever become so involved with any man again. Not that any man could compare with Alexander.

An unnerving sensation seared the pit of her belly and she set her briefcase on the marble tiles resolutely.

Don't think about the future. One step at a time. One day at a time.

But Alex wasn't giving up. "We could work with the publicity rather than against it."

Standing beneath an authentic French classic chandelier, Natalie angled slowly back. "Are you forgetting where this all started? There's a woman who's alone and carrying your baby."

His eyes glinted. "That's not been determined."

"Then perhaps you ought to help organise some tests."

She hated being snarky, but talk of buying multi-millionaire dollar mansions or taking advantage of bad publicity wouldn't help the situation.

"I spoke with a friend this morning," Alex said. "Mateo's a leading OB/GYN."

Her ears pricked. He'd spoken of Mateo Celeca before. Alex and the doctor had been fast friends since high school.

"After samples are taken from both Bridget and myself, we should have the results of the paternity tests within a week."

A wave of light-headedness swept over her.

If he was the father of that baby, they, as a couple, really would be over. No more acceding to games like today's. He would need to be with Bridget Davidson and her baby. No way would Natalie place herself in the middle.

She reclaimed her detached air. "Then it's going to be an intense week for you," she said, starting up the stairs.

"With the publicity it will be for you, too…unless we make the best of a bad situation."

She continued up the staircase.

"From the activity at Phil's," he went on, "I'm guessing your office was flooded with calls this morning. Celebrity does that."

"That's a steep price for a few leads. And when Phil realizes what's going on," that she was wasting her time here because this expedition was merely a way for Alex to get her alone and vulnerable, "I might not have a job."

"My bet is, after today he'll give you a big fat bonus."

Still ascending, she clapped one thigh. "Well, of course! Being involved with a man who is supposedly marrying one woman while another is having his baby is clearly something to endorse."

"Not everyone believes that two people who aren't suited to each other should marry for the sake of the child. It's a recipe for resentment and discord."

"There's a lot of old-fashioned folk who believe they should at least try." The folk back in Constance Plains, for instance. Bunch of small-minded hypocrites.

And, dammit, she wouldn't think about that, either.

She was halfway up the staircase when, as if by magic, he appeared before her, his powerful frame blocking her path. "And an equal amount of people would say I'm a man of principle for not going back on my word to you."

Her heart pounded as he loomed over her. He was everything a man should be. A powerhouse of raw conviction and simmering sexuality.

And, she had to remember, he was no longer hers.

"There's just one teensy problem. We weren't, aren't and never will be engaged. It's a lie."

"We can turn it into the truth."

She made an impatient sound then wound up around him. But he clasped her hand and she was tugged back to face his steely gaze.

"I can't do anything about Bridget's claim," he said. "Or that word is out we're to be married. If I retract that statement now, I'll look like an even bigger heel." His brows knitted. "Zhang knows about my grandfather's less than scrupulous reputation. Yesterday I convinced him that any investment would be safe with me. I told him I was a man of my word."

"An honourable man who carries through on his promises," she murmured, continuing his thread and hating that it'd begun to make some kind of sense.

This fake engagement had a business angle? Business implied impartiality, controlled feelings, calculated decisions.

And none of that meant she would go along with it.

"Cute plan," she offered, "but I'm sure you're aware of its flaws."

He nodded grudgingly. "Zhang's decision might not be affected by this story either way. On the other hand, if that newspaper report has swayed his opinion, perhaps nothing will swing it back. But even if Zhang doesn't go through with this deal, I'll have gained something more important." His foot found the higher stair and he leaned in close. "A wife."

Her eyes popped.

Wife!

She choked on a disbelieving laugh. "Whoa. Alex, listen to me. We are *not* engaged."

Deaf, *determined,* he dug into his back pocket and presented a small velvet box, then sprang open the lid.

The strength in her legs dissolved. A huge solitaire diamond glittered up at her. She'd never seen a stone that big, that dazzling. That perfect!

A bubble of emotion caught in her throat. She swallowed before it went to her head.

This scenario was all wrong, from beginning to end. She couldn't be engaged to him. She certainly couldn't *marry* him. He was probably the father of another woman's baby. Even if the tests came back negative, Tallie Wilder wasn't exactly prime wife material. Not if the man concerned wanted a family.

Alex had made it clear that having a son and heir was a priority, and she couldn't have another child. He wanted his wife's reputation to be above reproach. In her hometown, her name was synonymous with scandal.

And there was something else. Alex hadn't mentioned the reason a couple usually became man and wife. Oh, he desired her, enjoyed her company, treated her like a queen. But he didn't love her.

A lifetime ago she'd dreamed of love where no sacrifice was too great. Where what mattered above all else was the other person's feelings, security and trust. She'd imagined knowing the kind of love where forfeiting your most prized possession would be the least you could do if it eased your sweetheart's pain just a little.

Then she'd lost her baby as well as any emotion, other than grief and regret. Having known Alexander had brought her back to life. She still believed in that unique kind of love, maybe even for herself. She certainly wouldn't marry without it.

But while she felt sure Alex would make a wonderful, committed father, she wasn't certain he was capable of that kind of unconditional affection where a woman was concerned. To a shrewd man like Alex, deep romantic love would equal vulnerability, Samson and Delilah style. She had only to remember how coolly he'd relayed the standards he'd accept in a wife, or his suggestion a moment ago that they follow through with the engagement primarily because of business, to be sure of that.

He wanted the ideal wife and mother and he'd chosen her. What a joke.

Needing to escape—needing to breathe—she jogged back down the stairs. "Alex, don't do this."

"Because you had a more romantic offer in mind?"

Her heels clicking again on the vestibule tiles, she made a beeline for the door and tried to dissuade him with what was clear. "We've known each other three months."

"I'm looking forward to getting to know each other more."

If he knew about her pregnancy, he'd be running rather than chasing. That night six years ago still haunted her. The thought of dredging up all those hopeless, horrible feelings, then having him walk out, made her insides churn enough to retch.

Why couldn't he simply forget this crazy plan? Why wouldn't he accept her decision?

"I won't go along with a fabricated engagement to prove you're a man of your word."

"Then do it for the obvious reason. Because we belong with each other."

He didn't know what he was talking about. How could he belong with a woman who couldn't bear children? She might as well not be a woman at all.

The finality of that knowledge hit again, winding her like a medicine ball to the stomach. She stopped at the door, one hand on the doorjamb, the other on her midriff while tears filled her throat.

At her back, two hands cupped her shoulders as his hard frame pressed in.

"*Carino*, would it be so bad being married to me?"

She swallowed back emotion. "That's not the question you should be asking."

"Then what?"

Her throat thickened more. "You could very well be the father of that baby and you don't know?"

His fingers clamped her shoulders more before his hands lowered.

"There's more to this, isn't there?" he asked, and she froze.

Did he know something about her past?

"I think I understand," he ground out, "and I admit it might not be what you'd hoped for in a marriage… regularly caring for another woman's child as if it were your own."

Natalie blinked several times and slowly turned. Her voice was an incredulous whisper.

"You'd want me to help look after the baby?"

Engagements, marriage…she hadn't thought ahead to visitation or shared custody if the baby was his. She shouldn't now because what he proposed was impossible. She'd already inadvertently caused the death of one child. She shouldn't be responsible for another baby, even part-time.

A palm against her sick stomach, she shook her head again. "You don't know what you're saying."

His eyes dimmed more. "You don't like children?"

"I *adore* them."

"You don't think you could love a child that's not yours?"

Oh Lord. "That's not the problem."

Finding her hands, he clasped them to his chest. "We'll have our own children."

Her throat ached so much, she could barely find her voice. "And that's what you want, isn't it Alexander?" What you need. A son. An heir.

"Do you know what I want?" His dark penetrating eyes searched hers. "I want you."

She let go that breath.

He'd said *want*, not love, two totally different things.

But if she accepted this proposal, she would be a part-time mother of a child. Alexander Ramirez's child. She'd given up all hope…

Her heart squeezed.

She shouldn't even think such a thing. And just where would a marriage to Alex leave the unwed mother? Surely Bridget Davidson would want to marry the father of her child, particularly when the man concerned was Alexander.

And what of his suggestion that they have children of their own? *Impossible.*

Pressing the heel of her hand against her pulsing temple, she tried to think straight. There seemed a thousand ways this could go, but with only one likely outcome.

Someone would be hurt.

She shook her head, harder this time. "It won't work."

"Give me one good reason."

Everything. "It's all…too big of a gamble."

"Life's a gamble."

She sighed.

How would he react if he knew he'd proposed to a woman who was considered trailer trash back home? Who'd fallen pregnant then had inadvertently caused a miscarriage. Lump on top of that the fact she was now barren and he'd hit the jackpot in women *not* to marry.

He wanted her?

He wanted only what she'd been willing to show of herself to the world.

He changed the subject.

"What's your opinion on this house?" he asked, looking around.

Preoccupied by her thoughts, her reply was an automatic response. "I think it's a stunning investment that will only increase in value."

"You'd live here?"

"A sheikh would be happy living here."

"Then contact the owners."

Stunned, she stared at him. "That's crazy."

"You told me this is a good investment."

"Haven't you heard? Real estate agents aren't known for their integrity," she said pointedly.

His gaze intensified. "I shouldn't trust you?"

A strange calm fell over her and she knew if she told him about her past now, everything would change in an instant. He could do way better. He just didn't know it yet.

And the more sensible part of her—the part that adored him—didn't want him to know.

"And if I said you shouldn't trust me?" she asked.

"Then I'd have to go with gut instinct."

She didn't have time to think, to move. His strong arms were already around her, drawing her near, holding her against the pillar of the wholly masculine frame. The tips of their noses touching, he looked into her eyes, into her soul. She saw a fire flicker in their depths, then that familiar hunger and conviction leap and darken the irises more.

Time wound down as his mouth descended over hers. Her lips parted and then...

Then she was released. Or was that condemned? As he pressed closer, his tongue edging over and around hers, the kernel of desire low at her core condensed more, pulsing, burning, urging her to surrender reason and simply be.

When he gradually drew away, his eyelids were heavy, his breathing, too.

"I don't regret my slip last night to that reporter," he said, "because it crystallised in my mind what I want. I want a home, Natalie. It's time I settle down. We're good together. It can work."

She had to push him away. Tell him now how blind and mulish he was. Instead her fingers kneaded his chest.

"Don't do this." He was making her head spin, working his charm until she barely knew which way was up.

His shoulders rolled back. "Wear my ring."

Since the day they'd met, her life had seemed surreal. Men of Alexander Ramirez's calibre didn't inhabit her world, not the world of backwoods Tallie Wilder, anyway. When her baby had gone to Heaven that night, she'd given up on herself. She hadn't wanted happiness. She hadn't deserved it.

And yet how could she deny what she felt for Alexander? He helped fill that bleak cold hole inside her. When she was with him it was as if the shroud she'd worn for six years was, in part, removed.

Her more rational side knew there could be no engagement. The baby would be his and when he laid eyes on his child, Alex's protective nature would win out and he would *want* to marry Bridget. Be with his child. And if Bridget needed persuading, he'd do that, too. How could she—the 'other woman'—condemn them? Natalie only wished it was her.

"Phone the owners."

She blinked back from her thoughts. He was still on about the house.

"It's getting late now in Chicago," she told him.

"I doubt they'll mind having their dinner disturbed."

She gauged the tilt of his mouth.

Hell, he was really serious. And if he truly wanted this house, she shouldn't talk him out of it. There would simply be a different mistress living here than the one he imagined now.

But, given her shaky state, how well would she conduct an overseas call that potentially meant many thousands of dollars in commission for Phil's?

She studied his implacable expression again and sighed.

Guess she'd find out.

Twenty minutes later, the delighted vendors agreed to Alex's negotiated eight point seven-five million offer and had said to fax through the documents to their lawyer.

Thrilled, and a little shocked, Natalie slipped her cell phone into her briefcase. "That has to be the easiest sale I've ever made."

"And now I'd like to see the rest of my investment."

Her eyebrow lifted. "A little back to front."

"Whatever works."

Given she'd made a healthy commission and the

Quintons were ecstatic, she couldn't argue. She'd simply need to put the other, unrealistic matter out of her mind. Engagements, the possibility of being a part-time mother…

It wasn't happening.

Gathering herself, she waved toward the back of the house. "Let's start with the kitchen."

"I'm not a cook. I want to see upstairs."

He purposely brushed past and started up the stairs.

She tightened her lips. Damned if she'd give him the satisfaction of arguing. Irrespective of any ulterior motive he might have, she was acting as the Quinton's agent. She had to comply and show the new owner the second story. No matter what he threw at her, no matter what he said or did, she must remain professional.

When they reached the top of the stairs, she kicked off her commentary.

"There's four bedrooms on this floor, each with their own sitting room. There are two more bedrooms downstairs as well as a separate quarters on the grounds for live-in staff."

He was ducking his head around a bedroom doorway. "This looks nice."

Natalie followed. The guest room. Her favourite room.

"It was newly decorated before the Quintons left for overseas." She was drawn by the smell of freshly laid carpet and breathtaking scenery visible beyond the fall of exquisitely designed pelmets and drapes. "These views are as stunning as the main bedroom's." In fact, better, she thought. "You can see the bridge from here, the long blue stretch of harbour. And the breeze through these windows when they're open—"

A click sounded at her back. Her stomach fluttered and she swung around.

The door was shut and Alex was strolling toward her, his step deliberate. The gait of a man in no doubt about what he wants or to what lengths he'll go to attain it.

Natalie slid back one foot. "Alex, what are you doing?"

"The contract, once signed, is unconditional. This house, this bedroom, is as good as mine."

Quivering at the hungry gleam in his eye, she backed up more. "This is inappropriate."

"That's an interesting word. I'd have said inevitable."

Of course she'd known he'd planned this ambush of sorts. However, "If you think I'll let you undress me, here, in the middle of the day—"

"And make love to you long and hard?" He undid a shirt button. "Yes, *carino,* I think you'll let me."

The back of her legs hit the bed. He joined her and, without invitation, pulled the single clip from her hair then unzipped the back of her dress. Her more rational side silently protested, but she didn't stop him. Simply stated, at her most basic level, she wanted this and Alexander knew it as well as she did.

"You honestly don't have any shame, do you."

He peeled the dress from her shoulders. "Not where you're concerned."

He kissed her deeply and when her mind was wheeling, he skimmed his mouth down her neck, her cleavage, until his teeth grazed the gauzy fabric of her lace crop top bra. She bit back a cry as her nipples hardened against his mouth and her dress fell in a puddle at her feet.

His fingers wound into the scarlet lace and, in one fluid movement, he stripped the top up over her head. With obvious appreciation, he took time to study her breasts, weighing their fall as the pads of his thumbs brushed and teased the tips. When his head lowered again and his tongue twirled over one burning nipple, then the next, she sighed and her neck rocked back.

She was on fire.

Eyes drifting shut, she held his head in place. "Is the door locked?"

"No."

He sucked the sensitive bead fully into his mouth and a searing fountain fizzed through her veins. Still, her gaze edged toward the door.

"This doesn't feel right."

"Liar." As if he owned her—and at that moment he did—he scooped his hand down the front of her lace hipster shorts. "We always feel right together."

His other hand supporting her spine, he tipped her back and she sank into the silky spread. One knee on the mattress, he took hold of her last item of clothing. His absorbed gaze travelled all the way up her perpendicular legs to her pointing toes as he eased her hipsters off.

He brought her feet down and set them on the mattress a little apart. When a feather-light kiss brushed her inside thigh, she involuntarily bucked and whimpered.

She felt so alight. And exposed.

"At least draw the curtains."

He chuckled, a deep throated sound that let her know he was enjoying her show of modesty.

"You know I love your body. The way you feel, the way you look." The warm tip of his tongue trailed across her bikini line. "The way you taste."

When his mouth dipped more and he kissed her there, tenderly at first then more boldly, she arched and reached to knot her fingers in his hair.

He knew her weakness. Knew how to make her fly.

She hadn't had many lovers, but she knew enough to be certain his style was natural, a talent that was as innate as soaring and hunting were to a hawk.

When he touched her, loved her, her cares evaporated into mist. Where they were didn't matter. She only longed to feel his hard heat pressed close.

She wove her fingers through his silky hair. "When are you going to take your clothes off and join me?"

His only reply was the skilled attention of his circling tongue.

She sighed.

No one had a right to be this good.

The spiral climbed quickly and she wet her lips. "Alex...come up here."

His hands wove up her stomach and sculpted over her breasts, his thumbs and forefingers rolling until the concentrated sensations were so bright and powerful she could have wept. Her head lolling to the side, she groaned as her core compressed tighter around a deepening pulse.

Then, for two suspended beats, there was that eye-of-the-storm calm before her climax ignited and flung her to the stars. Biting her lip to stem a cry, she gripped the quilt at her sides as her mind and body exploded with raw pleasure that seemed to go on forever.

When finally the contractions wavered and began to die, drained, elated, tingling and never more sated, she didn't have the energy to move. She was barely aware that he'd left her until she dragged open her eyes.

He stood watching her, telling her with his eyes that she was his. Only his.

She held out her arms to him. He kicked off his shoes, discarded his clothes and extracted a condom from his wallet. When they were protected, he threw back half the quilt and scooped her up in his arms.

"This will be our room," he said, laying her on the cool sheet and nuzzling into the sweep of her neck.

When his body covered hers, she jumped, still so sensitive as he slid partway in and began to move.

He pressed a lingering kiss to her brow. "You will wear my ring."

Looping her legs around his thighs, she ran her fingertips over the hot damp mound of his back. "I can't think now."

"I don't want you to think. I want you to feel."

He thrust again, bumping her closer to a second orgasm. "My ring, Natalie."

Whether it was his bone-melting heat sliding against her or the dark-chocolate voice at her ear, in that moment he convinced her. This *was* their house, their new beginning. She *did* feel, and she felt wonderful. So utterly right she was dizzy with the magic of it.

She groaned as that spiral rose higher, squeezed tighter.

"Yes," she murmured.

Please, just...

Yes.

His mouth slanted over hers.

As fireworks flared again, she held him close and let the tidal wave swallow them both whole.

Six

After returning to work for a couple of hours, she and Alex spent the night together. The next morning Natalie headed home.

Not that she liked referring to Constance Plains in those terms. But she'd grown up there, had built her first dreams there. Constance Plains was where her mother lived and where a piece of Natalie's heart would always remain. Going back was hard, but also somehow cathartic.

In a strange, sad way, going home was sacred.

On the final isolated stretch of highway, zipping past the landscape of scattered gums and kangaroo grass, she selected a favourite CD. But even cranked up urban couldn't drown out the concerns that had tumbled through her mind since the weekend's astounding run of events.

Her gaze drifted to her left hand holding the wheel. The setting was dazzling, any girl's dream engagement ring, a cushion-cut single white diamond of who knew how many carats. Alex had been so persuasive about her wearing it. In hindsight she'd never stood a chance of refusing him. His reserves of sex appeal and charm exceeded any man she'd met or was ever likely to meet in the future.

Truth was she was attached to Alexander, hopelessly drawn to his intensity, as much as air was sucked into a fire or rain was absorbed by the sea. More and more he consumed her, but he also made her feel…connected.

As a smile touched her lips, a ray of morning sun caught the rock and the diamond flashed, shooting a stab of light back from the steering wheel. Squinting, Natalie shielded her eyes at the same time a truck roared up out of nowhere, its monster horn blasting as it passed.

Instinctively she yanked the wheel. The car swerved, fishtailing and skidding to the shoulder of the road. Foot to the floor on the brake, she pictured her heart hammering in her chest as every speck of mortal strength rushed down her rubbery legs and the car jolted to a stop. Dumping a head-tingling breath, she dropped her forehead on the wheel.

Remarkably she didn't think about her near collision. She could think only of the incredible moment Alex had slipped that ring on her finger.

Alex cared for her. He sincerely wanted her to be the mother of his children. But he didn't know anything about her. Didn't know she could never give him a legitimate heir. On top of that, his marriage proposal had a side agenda: publicly recanting the engagement might do his dealings with Mr. Zhang more harm than good.

Then again, she'd had a side agenda, too—a baby who might someday, in some measure, look upon her as a mother.

Dragging her brow off the wheel, she studied the stone on her third finger again. Today May Wilder would learn that her daughter had agreed to marry, and that her fiancé hadn't the faintest idea about her past.

Was she leaving it too late to pull out?

Releasing a shaky breath, she rolled her tense shoulders and swung back onto the highway. Thirty minutes later her Rav 4 veered into her mother's drive, on either side of which sat a sagging chain mail fence.

May must've heard the engine. By the time Natalie walked from the cracked cement drive to the house, May was standing on the porch, wiping her hands on a red-striped tea towel.

A heartfelt smile lighting her face, her mother flipped the towel over her shoulder and extended her arms. Relishing the comforting warmth, Natalie burrowed her face in her mother's shoulder, wishing her father were here, too.

After a long moment, May pulled back, her grey eyes glistening with unbridled love and pride. "You look so well, Tallie."

Natalie smiled. "So do you."

But in truth her mother's hair looked frizzy and her shoulders were slightly stooped. In her mother's eyes Natalie recognized again what she'd seen last visit. She was lonely. When her father died, she'd asked May to come live with her but she'd stoutly refused. This is where her life with Jack had been, May had said. She wouldn't leave, no matter what.

Now with her usual brave face, May linked an arm through her daughter's and swung open the screen door. "I put a roast on for lunch. The potatoes are browning."

Natalie stepped into the tidy living room. Fresh snapdragons fanned from a vase on the TV, the same washed out landscape paintings hung on the wall. The surroundings were reassuring yet unsettling, too.

Memories in every corner.

Bringing herself back, Natalie nodded. "A roast sounds great." Smelled great, too.

"Was it an easy drive from Sydney?"

"A breeze," Natalie fibbed as May crossed to flick on the air-cooler and she sank onto the couch.

"I have your room ready in case you'd like to stay over."

"Sorry. Can't. Work tomorrow."

"Well, the invitation's always there."

Crossing back, her mother's gaze landed on her daughter's hand, on the ring, and she hesitated before folding down beside her. Natalie had purposely kept the ring on so she couldn't back out of confessing. But now her stomach looped in guilty knots. She was not looking forward to this talk. It reminded her of a past conversation, only this time she wasn't the girl who'd got in trouble.

Smoothing down her skirt, Natalie siphoned in a steadying breath. "There's something I need to tell you."

"About Alexander Ramirez?"

Natalie's brows hitched. "The story made the local paper?"

May's smile was wry. "We do get the city paper way out here in the sticks."

"As far as I remember, you weren't interested in either."

"My neighbors are."

"Of course. I should've seen the smoke signals spreading the news when I drove in."

Despite Natalie's sarcasm, her mother smiled and held her hand. "He looks very handsome."

"He's…" Natalie swallowed the word *nice*, then *decent*. They didn't seem to fit.

"He's very good to me."

"I'm sure he is."

"He's what's known as a venture capitalist. They invest in other people's ideas."

"There was a small write-up about that, too."

Natalie nodded, stalling, trying to find the right words. Her mother wouldn't bring up the other information contained in that article, the claim that another woman was pregnant with Alexander's baby.

May Wilder would stick by her daughter under any and every circumstance, but Natalie couldn't bear to think about the added stares and whispers her mother would endure from this town's population after this. Whispers about that Wilder girl getting herself into strife again.

Natalie rearranged her hands in her lap.

"You know it's not certain that Alexander's the father of that child," she finally said, and her mother blinked several times.

"Oh? The reporter seemed sure."

Natalie huffed. The reporter was a slimeball.

"Alex has a friend, a doctor, who says paternity can be determined quickly."

May tipped closer. "I want you to remember, this isn't your fault. You wouldn't have agreed to marry him if you'd known."

At a twinge of shame, Natalie dropped her eyes. "It's a little more complicated than that."

But how could she explain? How would it sound?

I am wearing a man's ring when he knows nothing about my past, that I can't bear his children. I know I have to tell him and when I do that will be the end. But I can't help thinking about that baby, about giving her the love I wasn't able to give my own.

Natalie's nose stung at the threat of tears at the same time May's arms wrapped around her.

Her mother didn't speak for the longest time, but when she did it was in a supportive tone that tugged at Tallie's heart. "You don't have to go through with it if you don't want to."

She clamped her burning eyes shut. Her mother didn't understand. Natalie wasn't sure *she* understood.

Her mother's voice lowered more. "Do you love him?"

She thought it through. She loved her parents, she'd loved her baby. After that horrible black day six years ago, she'd never wanted to love anyone again. She hadn't thought she was capable.

"Alexander and I…we get on very well," she murmured truthfully.

"That's always a good sign."

"He treats me like a lady."

Her mother's smile was reminiscent. "So he should."

"He doesn't know…doesn't know about—"

She bit her lip, damming the sudden rush of emotion.

Her mother hugged her daughter tighter. "Tallie, you were always a good girl. Even good girls can take a wrong turn."

But Natalie pulled away and growled. She was sick of feeling seventeen.

"I wish I could go back." If only she hadn't stumbled that day. If only her baby had lived. God, she'd felt so *helpless*. "I wish I could squeeze all the horrible memories from my mind. Sometimes I think I have. But I've only ever pushed them down."

"It was God's will."

"Then why do I feel so responsible?"

"Because you're a deeply caring person who has a wonderful heart. That's why I believe in you. Why I've always believed."

Wrung out, Natalie searched her mother's gentle gaze. "If the baby *is* his, Alex should marry the mother of his child…shouldn't he?"

Not me.

Not even when she could already feel that dear baby in her arms. Knew the lullabies she would sing.

Her mother's mouth tightened. "Do you know what I really think?"

She shook her head. "Tell me."

May held her daughter's flaming cheek and Natalie saw that her mother's eyes were edged with tears. But then May smiled and stood, urging Natalie to her feet as well.

"I think we need a strong cup of tea." Bright again, May showed her only child to the kitchen. "After lunch, we'll see darling Mrs. Heigle over the road. She loves your visits, too."

The sun was a shimmering orange ball melting into the horizon by the time Natalie headed out of town.

After kissing her mother goodbye, she'd gone to spend an hour beneath the graceful umbrella of that poinciana tree. Following tradition, she replaced last month's soft toy—a small pink bear—with a new toy, a purple poodle puppy. Then she'd sat on the grass, gazed at the headstone, saying nothing.

Only wishing.

Now, as she cruised by the faded sign that read, Visit Constance Plains Again Soon, a car passed her coming in and Natalie did an unconscious double take.

Nothing unusual about the vehicle—your everyday, run-of-the-mill four-wheel drive. It was the glimpse of the driver that niggled. She wasn't sure why until ten miles out when the fleeting snapshot she'd caught gelled with the information knocking at her brain.

But then she laughed, shook her head.

That driver had ginger hair, yes. Didn't mean he was the reporter from the other night. Even if he, or anyone else for that matter, had wanted information on her, Internet and phones would be far quicker than an eight-hour round-trip like the one she'd complete today.

Which reminded her.

Natalie selected a CD then, settling into her seat, stifled a yawn.

She wouldn't reach Sydney until around nine. After a couple of restless nights, she couldn't wait for her head to hit the pillow. Even thoughts of Alexander and their uncertain future wouldn't ward off the Sandman tonight.

Her limbs were aching weights when, hours later, she steered into her apartment block's driveway. With a heavy arm, she swiped her keycard and the automatic gates leading to the underground car park rumbled up. Then something in the shadows caught her eye. A car, and this time the model was highly distinctive.

Sleek black Audi R8s weren't so run-of-the-mill.

Suddenly alert, she steered her car beneath the gate and swerved into her park. By the time she collected her bag off the passenger seat, Alexander stood by her door, reaching for the handle. A moment later, his warm hand gripped her elbow to help her out.

His face was dark and voice curiously gravelled. "It's after nine. I was beginning to worry."

A part of her was touched by his concern, but a bigger, thoroughly ragged part was slightly peeved.

"No need," she said, winding casually out of his hold. She'd been doing that drive for six years and she'd continue to do it for another sixty.

Then, through her exhaustion and jolt of his unexpected appearance, the obvious question dawned.

She studied him more closely. "Alex, why are you here?"

Was something wrong with Bridget…with the baby?

"It's been a crazy day," he said, walking with her to the lift, his eyes cast down. "I've needed to make some decisions. Decisions that affect you."

"Is Bridget all right?"

"I spoke with her briefly. Mateo said he'd fit her in anytime, but it was hard pinning her down to a day." He stabbed the lift's call button. "She said she wishes none of this had happened. She apologised for dragging me into it."

Her heart dropped more. Bridget Davidson sounded sweet. Someone who deserved a good man as well as a nice life for herself and her baby. Natalie almost felt she knew her.

She found her voice over the stone stuck in her throat. "I'm sure you told her that you feel as responsible as she does."

He slid over a look. "As I've said before, if I'm responsible, I'll be there for them both, no question."

After they stepped into the lift, Alex closed his eyes and rubbed his brow while Natalie pressed her floor's button and a warning tingling stole up over the back of her scalp.

He looked so preoccupied. So drawn. Was she jumping to conclusions or was the decision he'd made today concerning her linked to his last statement? Was he here to tell her that he'd had a change of heart? Perhaps after his discussion with Bridget today he'd decided that, if the baby was his, he'd be there for them in more than a single-parent, part-time kind of way.

It shouldn't be a surprise. Alex staying with the mother of his child was the morally right thing to do. She couldn't forget how Chris Nagars had run out on his responsibilities. He'd turned his back, not only on her but also on the baby she'd carried.

She turned her face toward the wall.

Then again, she was no angel. She'd had her own reasons for kidding herself and accepting Alex's ring. Fact was, Alex should focus on Bridget and that baby now, and they both knew it.

"I spoke with your boss today."

She straightened and concentrated on his words. Alex had spoken to Phil? "About the Quinton house?"

"In part. Given you were unavailable, I asked him to arrange for the contract to accommodate rent before handover."

"You plan to move in straightaway?"

"Yes, I do. With you."

Her breath caught. One minute he was announcing he would be there for Bridget. Now he'd decided to move in with the other woman?

She raked a trembling hand through her hair. "I don't suppose you considered asking me first?"

"Not after seeing the six o'clock news."

She studied the hard edge to his mouth, the penny dropped and a withering feeling fell through her.

"I don't believe it," she murmured, cringing at the thought of having their private lives highlighted on prime-time TV. "Don't they have better things to report on?"

"Apparently not. They even found some vision of my grandfather in his heyday." His frown deepened. "A camera crew was waiting outside this building until thirty minutes before you pulled up. I thought they might've gone to hunt you down…" He gave a thankful grin. "Anyway, you're safe. But you can bet they'll be back and they won't be gracious."

Retrieving a key from her bag, Natalie crossed to her

apartment's front door. His protective instincts were laudable but clearly Alex hadn't thought this through.

"Even if I move out of here, they could still corner me at work if they want to."

"You don't need to go to work."

She stopped to slant her head at him. "I beg your pardon?"

"You're on vacation. I organised it with Phil."

Dumbfounded, she coughed out a humourless laugh. "*Phil*, now, is it?"

"He agreed that it's best you take time off."

She set her jaw.

Not tired, not compassionate. Now she was angry.

"Do I get any say in this? I mean, has anyone heard of dialing a mobile phone? I think you have my number."

"I didn't want to upset you when you had such a long drive to get through. You have enough on your mind."

"An understatement," she mumbled, threading her key into its lock.

He followed her inside, his tall masculine build looking out of place in her single bedroom unit. "For the time being, it's best."

Says Alexander Ramirez.

She tossed her keys on the hallstand and, her back to Alex, pressed her clasped hands to her waist.

She was ticked off that Alex had spoken with Phil without her consent, but it had gone beyond that. Her boss thought having her lay low for a while was a good idea. Phil wasn't a pushover. He wouldn't have agreed if he hadn't been certain. Perhaps he thought the initial boost the publicity had given *Phil's* might ultimately turn sour.

These days people wanted heroes more than ever. Given the perceived moral dilemma here—a man marrying one woman while getting another pregnant—potential customers might take a stand and look elsewhere for their property needs.

She owed her boss a great deal. And she hadn't had a vacation in…was it two years? This minute she was exhausted, mentally, physically, totally spent.

Leaning against the wall, she heeled off her shoes.

Hell, why fight it? Maybe a few days off wasn't such a bad idea.

Not wanting to give in too easily, she headed for the kitchen. "How long have you men decided I should take off?"

"Phil said to take as long as you need."

Feeling suddenly chilled, she crossed and rubbed her arms. "He wants me back, right?"

"With a huge sale like you made yesterday?" She heard him grunt. "I don't think that's in dispute."

"That sale had nothing to do with my ability."

"Don't underestimate yourself." He followed her to the corner of the kitchen where she reached for the kettle. "I was seriously in the market and you negotiated like a true pro. You'd be an asset on anyone's team. Including mine."

She looked over her shoulder. A lazy smile was tugging on his mouth. This man couldn't help being sexy if he tried.

She cocked an eyebrow. "I'm not in the market for another job."

"Oh, in my case, our affiliation would be purely personal."

When his arms ravelled around her, urging her to fully face him, half her fatigue melted away, to be replaced by far more inviting, provocative feeling. Still, she tried to look sternly at him. He got away with too much too easily.

She set her palms against his chest. "You're doing a charm job on me again."

"Is it working?" He nipped the sensitive shell of her ear and his warm breath stirred her flesh to goose bumps.

She sighed and her head rocked back. She was all out of fight.

"So where is this vacation taking place?"

"It's a surprise?"

"All right. So what do I need?"

"A few changes of clothing. Some after-five gear."

She quizzed eyes. "I thought we were going underground." Hiding from the press.

His grin was crooked. "There's all kinds of ways to dodge a bullet."

Seven

Natalie packed a few things and they made it back to Alex's new address without incident.

Clearly, though, the past few days had caught up with her. When Alex steered his Audi into the Quinton mansion—now the Ramirez Mansion—Natalie could barely keep her eyes open. He parked beneath the portico, as he'd done the day before, but when he opened the passenger-side door, in the moonlight, through sleepy eyes, she saw his brow descend.

"It's a good thing I stepped in when I did," he muttered, angling to scoop her off the seat and into the cradle of his capable arms. "If anyone needs a break, it's you."

She was leaden, almost too tired to protest, but she also had her pride. "You don't need to carry me."

Nevertheless, he did just that, bumping the car door shut with his hip then striding up the wide sandstone stairs that led to the grand front entrance. Without setting her down, he slotted the key, already in his hand, into the lock and carried her inside. But then he stopped and simply stood beneath that colossal French chandelier, as if waiting for some sign or sound while he silently dominated the deepening shadows.

Held so firmly against his chest, a strangely luminous sensation cascaded through her and Natalie took a moment to gather words to describe it.

Dreamlike, she thought. But, more so, *fated*. It was as if her whole life she'd waited for this man to carry her into this house when she would feel this way.

Close to peaceful.

Very nearly loved.

Did Alex feel the same?

Raising the arm that supported her legs, he flicked a switch. The chandelier lights flashed on, beaming crystal prisms around the vaulted vestibule. Alexander's dark eyes glittered as he studied her and the line between his brows deepened more.

"You really are shot, aren't you?"

Stifling a surprise yawn, she tried to shake herself awake. Now with the lights on, rather than peaceful she felt more like a sack of cement. Alex must think she felt as heavy as one, too.

She wriggled. "I'm fine, really. You can put me down now."

But he was busy regarding their current location in connection to the rest of the house. His gaze travelled up the stairs that led to the bedrooms, and she remembered yesterday when he'd coaxed her into that bedroom and how he'd made love to her in a way which had been both wonderfully familiar and yet different to any other.

She remembered how his mouth had trailed over her quivering belly, how his bristled chin had grazed the tips of her breasts. Finally she remembered how his muscular body had both pinned her down and simultaneously propelled her up into the clouds.

She stole a look at the set of his firm jaw and intense gleam in his eyes as he evaluated the stairs and, despite her exhaustion, Natalie's insides kicked in anticipation.

But then a rumble of decision sounded in his chest and he strode with her down a left-hand hall.

A moment later, they entered the exceptionally appointed theatre room. He flicked on the low wattage down lights then moved to lay her upon one

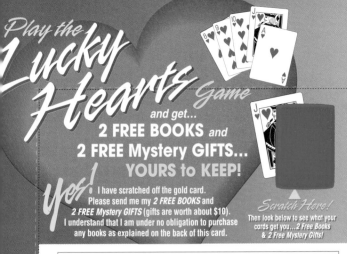

Play the Lucky Hearts Game

and get...
2 FREE BOOKS and
2 FREE Mystery GIFTS...
YOURS to KEEP!

Yes! I have scratched off the gold card.
Please send me my *2 FREE BOOKS* and
2 FREE Mystery GIFTS (gifts are worth about $10).
I understand that I am under no obligation to purchase
any books as explained on the back of this card.

Scratch Here!
Then look below to see what your
cards get you...2 Free Books
& 2 Free Mystery Gifts!

We want to make sure we offer you the best service suited to your needs. Please answer the following question:
About how many NEW paperback fiction books have you purchased in the past 3 months?
❑ 0-2   ❑ 3-6   ❑ 7 or more

326 SDL EZML   225 SDL EZMW

FIRST NAME   LAST NAME

ADDRESS

APT.   CITY

STATE / PROV.   ZIP/POSTAL CODE

Visit us online at
www.ReaderService.com

Twenty-one gets you
2 FREE BOOKS and
2 FREE MYSTERY GIFTS!

Twenty gets you
2 FREE BOOKS!

Nineteen gets you
1 FREE BOOK!

TRY AGAIN!

© 2009 HARLEQUIN ENTERPRISES LIMITED. Printed in the U.S.A.
® and ™ are trademarks owned and used by the trademark owner and/or its licensee.

▼ DETACH AND MAIL CARD TODAY! ▼

(S-D-09/09)

The Reader Service—Here's how it works:

Accepting your 2 free books and 2 free mystery gifts (gifts are worth about $10.00) places you under no obligation to buy anything. You may keep the b and gifts and return the shipping statement marked "cancel." If you do not cancel, about a month later we'll send you 6 additional books and bill you just $ each in the U.S. or $4.74 each in Canada. That's a savings of 15% off the cover price. It's quite a bargain! Shipping and handling is just 50¢ per book.* You cancel at any time, but if you choose to continue, every month we'll send you 6 more books. which you may either purchase at the discount price or return and cancel your subscription.

* Terms and prices subject to change without notice. Prices do not include applicable taxes. Sales tax applicable in N.Y. Canadian residents will be charged applic provincial taxes and GST. Offer not valid in Quebec. All orders subject to approval. Credit or debit balances in a customer's account(s) may be offset by any outstanding balance owed by or to the customer. Please allow 4 to 6 weeks for delivery. Offer available while quantities last.

If offer card is missing write to: The Reader Service, P.O. Box 1867, Buffalo, NY 14240-1867 or visit us at www.ReaderService.com.

BUSINESS REPLY MAIL

FIRST-CLASS MAIL   PERMIT NO. 717   BUFFALO, NY

POSTAGE WILL BE PAID BY ADDRESSEE

THE READER SERVICE
PO BOX 1867
BUFFALO NY 14240-9952

NO POSTAGE
NECESSARY
IF MAILED
IN THE
UNITED STATES

of five connected plush chaise lounges, set in a semi-circle aimed at a giant in-house screen.

Inwardly she sighed at his consideration but outwardly she challenged him. He was always so ready to take charge.

"I'm not an invalid," she explained.

Leaning over her, he brushed his warm lips against hers and growled, "Don't be stubborn. Tonight, *carino*, let me take care of you."

Her mouth swung to one side. In truth, she *was* shot, worn through to the bone and she might be resting on a pile of downy feathers, this chaise was so decadently soft.

"No argument?" He waited then, on a slanted grin, nodded once. "Good." He straightened and headed out. "I'll get your things from the car, make a phone call I can't put off and then…" He stopped at the doorway, rapped his fingers on the jamb and told her over the ledge of a broad shoulder, "Then we'll go to bed."

As he disappeared down the hall, Natalie nestled into the lounge, wishing this scenario was as simple as it might outwardly appear. She'd moved in with her handsome fiancé, a successful and respected man who treated her like a princess. But how long would the illusion last?

Another shuddering yawn consumed her. Her searching hand landed on the wool throwblanket splayed over the next chaise and she stuffed a portion of it under her head for a makeshift pillow. The rest she curled over her hip.

Some people lives were charmed. Others had the strength of will to overcome the toughest of trials. She'd faced life's worst, the death of a child. Now she was facing another challenge…the wait to see whether Alex was the father of Bridget's baby.

Were her instincts tonight right? Despite bringing her here to protect her from the media, if the paternity test proved positive, would Alex ultimately choose the traditional and honourable course? Would he choose to marry Bridget and be a full-time father to his baby?

Frowning, she burrowed more into her pillow.

No matter how strong their attraction for each other, no matter how much she craved his company, if he planned to stand by Bridget, she already understood and supported that decision more than he could ever know.

A heavy wave curled over her. She closed her eyes and began to drift.

And if Alex did choose Bridget, he would never need to know about her past. She would never need to have him look at her with an awful mixture of pity and futility.

The way she sometimes looked at herself.

When Natalie woke the next day her mind was clear and her body felt gloriously refreshed. Moving against the warm soft bedding, she took her sweet time opening her eyes.

The earliest mists of sunlight were slanting in through an opening in some curtains.

She rubbed her eyes and got her bearings.

Not her bedroom. Not Alexander's, either. Rather she was reclined in the Quinton's home theatre room. Last night he'd left saying he would return soon, but she must've dozed off.

Stirring more, she angled her head.

On the far chaise lounge, a quiet figure sat in the patchy light…a darkly attractive man, one elbow resting on the chaise arm, his curled knuckles supporting his strong shadowed jaw. He held something, was studying it intently. A small disc that he flipped over his fingers much like a gambler might flip a chip. He manoeuvred the—was it some kind of coin?—across and under his fingers, concentrating as if the action might reveal the secret that would unlock the mysteries of the world.

The flipping stopped.

As his head turned, a lock of blackest hair fell over his brow and Natalie's heartbeat skipped. His smile was soft, unreservedly masculine and at the same time sinfully beautiful.

He swung his legs onto the floor. "You're awake."

His chest was bare while Levi's hung like a dream on his lean hips. The button was left undone and as he strolled over she fought to keep her gaze from travelling down the arrow of crisp dark hair visible below his navel. Stopping before her, he rushed a hand through that fallen lock of hair and her stomach gave a pleasant twist.

He couldn't know how sexy he was. How his every movement made her skin heat and heart beat a little faster.

"Did you sleep well?" he asked in a deep husky voice that resonated through to her bones.

She stretched. Smiled. "I feel as if I've slept a hundred years."

"When I came back from my call, I didn't have the heart to wake you."

Despite her dilemma, she thought of that bedroom, of the blissful hours they'd spent beneath its sheets, and she only wanted to have him lift her in his arms again and kidnap her upstairs.

Wondering if her thoughts showed—in a way wishing they did—she inwardly sighed and straightened more. "Did you sleep down here, too?"

"A little."

He looked refreshed enough. Smelled fresh, too. But she guessed he'd had a shower and hadn't slept at all. That he'd spent the quiet hours of the night working the previous days' events over in his mind.

The piece in his hand caught the light and she tilted her head, trying to gain a better look. "What's that?"

"A family heirloom, believe it or not."

He opened his palm and revealed a worn coin with some sort of emblem on its uneven surface. "It looks ancient."

"It's a Spanish doubloon, minted in the days of Isabella and Ferdinand."

He made to drop it in her hand but she shrank back, hesitant to touch something so precious. It must be worth a fortune.

"I promise there's no ghosts attached," he told her. "Or none that I know of."

She studied the humor in his eyes then laughed at herself. It was just a coin, a very old, queer-looking coin. It wasn't as if she could lose it on him or anything. She put out her hand and the gold piece slid into the cup of her open palm.

It was warm from his touch and she tested its weight. "Heavy. And not at all round."

"Doubloons were made with an ounce of gold and minted by hand. It's been handed down from generation to generation. Passed on from Ramirez firstborn son to firstborn son."

So that's why he'd been examining it so intently. He'd been thinking that if Bridget's baby was his, if the baby was a boy, by virtue of tradition this coin should be handed down to him.

"It's presented to the eldest boy of each generation on his twenty-first birthday," he went on. "My parents made a big deal of it when they gave the coin to me. It was the first and only time I saw tears in my father's eyes."

He was peeling off his layers, letting her in, wanting her to see what truly lay beneath the tycoon's cool facade…a man who valued and respected his family, past and future.

Her fingers unfurled and she handed the coin back.

She wished she could give him that son. She wished she could see that same emotion Alex had seen in his father's eyes the day his boy had turned twenty-one. Pride. Devotion. A sense of immortality. She could only imagine.

The moment stretched as he studied the coin.

"That phone call I made last night," he finally said. "I contacted a numismatic auction firm. A coin dealer."

"You want to sell this?"

His flashing eyes jumped to hers. "Never. It will stay in the Ramirez family. It certainly won't leave my possession until my son is twenty-one."

Alexander had had his share of romantic affairs, but it was clear how he saw his future. Married with children, particularly a boy. A son who would accept this tangible reminder of who and what he was above all else.

A Ramirez.

"Then why did you contact a dealer?" she asked.

"To hunt down another coin in case…" He exhaled and cleared his throat. "If Bridget Davidson's baby is mine and a male, he ought to be acknowledged appropriately. But circumstances such as these…I don't know that it's happened before." His gaze bore into the doubloon. "I'd always envisaged this coin going to the son of the woman I married."

He pushed up tall and shrugged. "Unfortunately the dealer isn't hopeful of securing another. This specific type of doubloon is the most sought after coin in the world."

"Will you try another dealer?"

His eyes searched hers, dark and curious. "Do you think I should?"

He was torn between making the honourable choice should Bridget's child be his and facing the fact that the Ramirez doubloon might go to a son he might not raise, or not in the traditional sense anyway.

Was Alex wondering too whether Bridget would put Ramirez on the birth certificate? Perhaps by law the biological father could insist. If not it would mean the fall of a centuries-old tradition. That coin would no longer belong to the Ramirez name.

Her mind full of questions, Natalie put her weight on the floor and almost fell. Her leg was asleep.

She winced and held her calf, willing away the

tingling rash of pins and needles. "Guess I got too comfortable during the night."

He slipped the coin into his back pocket, hunkered down and rubbed, working the circulation back into her leg with careful ministrations.

After a moment, he asked, "How's that?"

"Better."

He kept rubbing. "Are you hungry?"

She hadn't eaten since her mother's baked custard late yesterday afternoon.

She smiled. "Now that you mention it."

"Good, because I have this driving urge to try out the new kitchen."

She narrowed her eyes. "I didn't think you were interested in ovens and hot plates."

"Oh, ye of little faith."

He couldn't be more wrong. "I have all the faith in the world." In him. That he'd do the right thing.

His gaze intensified, absorbing hers before he smiled a different smile, as if she couldn't have said anything to make him more pleased.

He took her hand and eased her up. "Let's christen the kitchen."

Despite her arguments, Alex refused help with breakfast. So Natalie followed his advice and enjoyed a lovely long shower. Twenty minutes later, feeling snug and smelling sweet in an oversized plush towelling robe, she wandered downstairs. She made her way into the kitchen, drawn by the aroma of, if she wasn't mistaken, mushroom omelette.

Seeing the "chef" busy at the giant island counter, she stopped, smiled and crossed her arms. "I'm impressed."

Alex's attention jumped from where he slaved over a sizzling hot plate. He twirled an imaginary moustache and drawled in a French accent, "I 'ave many 'idden talents."

She dropped her arms and laughed. "I don't doubt it." She moved forward as he sprinkled parsley into the pan. "Did you grocery shop before collecting me last night?"

"I've hired a housekeeper. Zelda McFinney came in yesterday to spring clean and fill the pantry and fridge."

She pretended to pout. "Does that mean I don't get to do your laundry?"

"Never."

By the look, he meant it, just as he'd meant his vow regarding the doubloon: he intended for it to stay in the Ramirez line. His *direct* line.

She pulled the sash tighter around her waist.

She couldn't avoid it. He was living a fairy tale if he thought she could help him do that. She'd have to confess and set him straight. But standing beneath the warm soft hiss of the shower, she'd had time to sort out the best time.

If she spoke to him now, Alex would have no choice. He wanted a family, children she wouldn't conceive, and so he would do what needed to be done. He'd say goodbye. She knew that. Accepted it. From the start she'd known they couldn't last.

However, she could make certain that they parted only after Alex had secured Zhang's support and no harm would come from gossip that their engagement was indeed off. And, with her out the way, he could revisit in another light the possibility of marrying Bridget if the paternity result proved positive.

Natalie was happy for Bridget's sake. She knew how she must feel. Alone. Happy about the baby yet worried, too. Every child deserved a full-time father.

Alex's bicep flexed as he scraped at the eggs, which had stuck to the frying pan. He growled. "Shouldn't it be easier than this?"

Despite her deeper thoughts, she smiled at the scene—a big, bronzed, half-naked man wrestling with his spatula.

Joining him, she put out her hand. "Here. Let me."

A moment later, she had the omelette flipped and ready to serve, although keeping her mind on the task hadn't been easy with Alex's dropping a seductive line of kisses up and down her neck the whole time.

"Mmm," he hummed near her ear. "You taste so good."

"Taste this."

She grabbed a fork, sliced off some omelette and, spinning, slid the tines between his lips. The surprise on his face morphed to satisfaction as he ran a fingertip across his top lip, pushing a stray morsel into his mouth.

"Whaddaya know. I can cook!"

She laughed and slipped omelette on two separate plates.

They sat at the breakfast table, early morning light streaming between the opened plantation shutters and glinting off the silverware.

Halfway finished, Natalie admitted, "This must be the best breakfast I've ever tasted."

The fork paused an inch from his mouth. "Are you telling me I get the job?"

"I wouldn't complain."

He swallowed that mouthful and reached for his juice. "My mother was top-notch in the kitchen, although when Teresa and I were older she was more a supervisor than hands-on."

"My mum's a pretty good cook, too," Natalie chipped in, remembering yesterday's baked spuds. But then she turned the conversation back to him, a trick she'd become expert at since living in Sydney. She liked to keep her background in the background and never more than now. "What about your father? Was he a hands-on type of dad?"

"The best. He was a musician, a genius on the classic guitar. Unfortunately, I, on the other hand, play like a farmhand with a banjo." They laughed together then he took a sip, swallowed and set his glass down. "What does your father like to do?"

Her heart constricted and she inhaled to tamp the pain. "He passed on two years ago."

His cutlery went down. "Natalie, I'm sorry. It's hard losing a parent."

He'd lost both father and mother. Not that he'd spoken about the circumstances. She understood. Talking about…those things was difficult.

"My dad played an instrument, too," she said, trying to recapture the lighter mood. "A piano accordion. He'd pump out a tune, tapping his heel while our terrier bounced in a circle on his hind legs."

He smiled and the emotion that reached his eyes touched her heart. "Sounds as if you had a happy childhood."

"I had everything I needed."

Plenty of food, a nice home, two parents who loved her and enough on paydays to cover the bills.

"What were you like as a teenager? The angel you are now or more an adolescent devil?"

She wiped her mouth on a napkin and tried to answer without answering. "You, I'm sure, were a saint."

At her tease, he rubbed his brow and chuckled. "We would've made a good pair, I think."

Regret for what she'd lost, and what she was yet to lose, sailed through her.

She smiled softly. "I think we'd've made a good pair, too."

He reached across the table to hold her hand. "And now?"

"And now…"

I simply want to spend the rest of my life with you. But she would have to be content with another day or two. A week if she were lucky. However long it took for Zhang to commit to Alex's current project. Then she'd tell him what he might not want to hear but would, nevertheless, need to accept.

Shunting the thought aside, she pushed to her feet and answered his question in a bright voice. "Now I think the washing up needs doing."

As she passed, he grabbed her robe's tie and tugged. "I'll be bitterly disappointed if you're not naked under this."

She lowered her face to his and murmured, "What if I am?"

He cupped her nape and brushed his lips over hers. "I'll be tempted to divulge another of my hidden talents."

Knowing he referred to his skill in the bedroom,

she assured him. "I think you've shown me everything there is to know."

He pressed a soft kiss to the side of her mouth. "*Carino,* you are so naïve."

Eight

She'd never made love on a kitchen chair before.

Guess I am a little naïve, she'd thought when Alex had stripped off her robe and coaxed her to straddle his lap. He'd left his jeans undone for a reason, and as he laved scintillating affection upon her shoulders, her neck, her breasts, she felt him harden more against her thighs.

Kneading her hips, he rumbled out a groan of deepest pleasure.

"Why can I never get enough of you?"

Shimmying beneath her, he shifted his jeans until his engorged shaft was released. After he'd found and fitted a condom, rather handy in his jeans back pocket, he lifted her slightly, and when he pressed her down, manoeuvring her against him again, his erection pushed and eased in.

Catching her breath, she coiled her arms about his broad neck and began to move with him…around him. Oh Lord, he felt so good.

Her mouth dropped to nip his ear. "Do you plan on taking me in every room?"

"I plan on enjoying you as often as I can."

"Every day."

"Every hour if I could."

In an effortless movement, he pushed to his feet. Her legs wrapped around his hips as he rested her back against the nearest wall. Holding her firm, he made love to her until, suddenly, he stilled and all the muscles in his steamy back hardened.

He eased out a long breath, continued to move, to grind and to shift. Then he hit a spot that made her gasp and burn for him all the more. His shoulders were slick with perspiration, his breathing evocatively heavy. She kissed his temple and his morning beard grazed her chin.

"I like being on holiday with you," he whispered.

But she couldn't reply. The passion had built to a point where she could only concentrate on the pulsing seed about to split apart and catch light.

"You're everything any man could ever want," he murmured against her hair, kissing her brow.

She wanted to agree. Wanted to forget anything existed but this moment. And so she held on, her mouth finding his, her ankles scissored behind him as he drove her closer, higher, harder...

She felt the muscles in his back bunch at the same time he filled her fully. She trembled at the rumble in his chest a second before she too was raised up and thrown over the edge.

A rolling wave of contractions gripped her, tingling through her veins, glowing and radiating out. Embracing each and every sensation, she buried her face against his strong corded neck and held on, feeling him throb, wanting him so much that tears stung behind her closed eyes.

This was far more than sex, always had been from their very first time. This moment she knew more clearly than ever...she was edging closer to falling in love with Alexander. And that was dangerous because being with him, having him all to herself, was not only too good to be true.

It was too good to last.

They were still floating down, holding each other, when, nearby, his cell phone buzzed. Feeling heavy, sated, she slowly brought her face away, found his eyes and smiled a dreamy smile.

His eyebrows fell in. "Don't think for a moment I'm getting that."

"It could be important."

"*This* is important."

"It could be your Mr. Zhang."

His brow pinched.

When she wriggled against him, he weakened and lowered her until her feet touched the cool tiled floor. He lifted his jeans with one hand while sweeping her robe off the floor with the other.

He threaded the sleeves onto her arms and she laughed. "Will you get the phone already?"

She prayed it was good news for him. Which meant bad news for her, and sooner than expected. But she couldn't think about that. She wanted Alex to succeed. In business. In life.

Yes, even in love.

He moved to collect the phone.

"Yes?" He nodded once, grunted. Then he shifted his weight and smashed his fist on the kitchen counter.

Jumping at the thump, she held her clasped hands at her throat. Was it Zhang? Had he said no? Or was this call to do with Bridget and the baby?

Alex shovelled fingers through his hair. "Get them the hell away from there." A pause. "I don't care how, just do it!"

He disconnected and practically threw the phone at the wall. Then he scowled at the counter for what seemed an eternity before she edged forward, almost too frightened to ask.

"What's happened?"

He inhaled sharply and looked at her. "They know we're here."

"They?"

"That was Paul. I'd asked him to keep an eye out. He cruised past and saw a reporter trying to scale the fence."

Suddenly light-headed, she sank into the nearby chair. "How did they know…?"

A leak at her office?

His determined onyx gaze narrowed. "We need to put a stop to this." He crossed over, kneeled before her and his warm hands found hers. "We'll make a statement to the press, they'll see we have nothing to hide, and then the world can leave us the hell alone."

Regret stuck like a pip in her throat. She only wished it were that simple. She wished he loved her and she could be the bride he needed. This wasn't a silly misunderstanding that could be cleared up over a decent one-on-one. She couldn't marry without love and Alex wouldn't marry without the promise of offspring. Nevertheless, it was a conversation they needed to have, even if her heart ached so much she felt she might die.

Her gaze fell away, but he curled a knuckle under her chin and forced her to look at him.

"I'll fix this and, no matter what—" She turned her head again but he turned it back. "No matter what," he repeated firmly, "you have my word, we will be married."

When she looked away a third time, Alex held that breath and slowly pushed to his feet.

Yes, she'd been upset over his unexpected statement to that reporter. She was torn, as was he, over Bridget Davidson's pregnancy. But she couldn't hide the way she felt for him. The same way he felt for her. They were perfect for each other in and out of the bedroom. She loved kids, they'd be happy. What more was there?

Why was she avoiding his eyes?

His heart crashing against his ribs, he uttered the words.

"Natalie, what aren't you telling me?"

Her shoulders were hunched, her head bowed. He watched as the dainty hand clutched her knee.

"Please…give me a moment," she murmured.

He blinked twice, wondering.

Aside from the first time, he'd worn protection whenever they'd made love. She couldn't be pregnant. She'd have known before this.

Still, if she thought that news would make him angry or upset, she was wrong. That wouldn't make his life harder. To the contrary, that event would cement his decision. They would be married, no delay.

He urged her up and gathered her close. "You can tell me, *carino*."

When she looked up, her eyes were edged with the sheen of unshed tears. "I didn't want to tell you."

His chest tightened. "You can tell me anything."

She nodded. Hesitated. Bit her lip.

"I understand how Bridget's feeling."

"I know you do."

"I know what it feels like to…to…"

He continued to hold her close but he didn't try to finish the sentence for her. Although he was certain now what she must want to say, she needed to say it in her own way. Then it was his job to comfort her and assure her that he was here for her and would always be—in a way he simply couldn't be for Bridget.

Natalie was special.

Beyond special.

She mumbled against his chest. "I've been pregnant."

He nestled his cheek against her crown and smiled as he'd never smiled before. It was as he'd thought. Soon he would have the child, the legitimate heir, he needed.

"You're pregnant," he murmured against her ear.

She shook her head and found his gaze. "I *was*

pregnant. I had a child, Alex. Six years ago when I was seventeen."

The world slid on its axis at the same time the circle of his vision seemed to close in. He blinked several times before, his hands on her shoulders, he stepped back to judge the expression in her eyes.

"You...have a child?"

Her eyes were wide. "I do. I *did*. She died...the night she was born."

His right hand fell back on the kitchen counter while his left held his brow as a thousand thoughts shot through his mind. She'd had another man's baby. The child was *dead?*

"The father?"

"When I told him I was pregnant," she said, "he left town. I haven't heard from him since."

Coward. Then another burning question. "Did you love him?"

"I thought I did. I was seventeen."

He blew out a breath.

Well, this changed everything. He knew what he wanted in a wife. He expected the woman he married, who bore his children, to have an unsullied past. Getting pregnant at seventeen did not fit the bill. What had her parents been thinking to have let this happen? What kind of home had she grown up in? She said she'd had everything she'd needed, and implied her childhood had been a happy one.

Had she been lying? After this revelation, how could he trust her?

She hadn't come from any circle that he knew. He should have done his research, but he hadn't expected their relationship to be anything more than a fling. Yet he couldn't deny it, his affection for her had grown. At what point had his feelings changed?

He shoveled a hand through his hair while Natalie gazed at the floor. His beautiful, fiery, fragile Natalie.

He scrubbed his jaw. To rail over this would be pointless. At seventeen she'd been little more than a kid who should have been protected. Still, some interesting information had come from her confession. One, she was fertile. Two, regardless of the past, he still wanted her, and if they were to be married, rather than sounding judgemental, he needed to be supportive.

Focusing on the here and now, he joined her again and held her in a different way, with more tenderness than he knew he owned. He traced his lips over her crown making noises he hoped would sooth. She was so stiff. He imagined the tears banked up in her throat.

So many little things made sense now. The way she'd reacted when Teresa had mentioned starting a family. The way she'd defended Bridget's position so fiercely.

"But we will have more children. As many as you want."

Closing her eyes, she slumped and shook her head. "You don't understand."

He thought of the doubloon. "Life is empty without family. Without children. You knew a moment of that kind of fulfilment six years ago. You'll know it again, and keep it, when we have our first."

Hopefully a son.

The expression in her eyes was almost blank. "What if I told you I don't see children of my own in my future?"

He set his forehead against hers. "Then I would tell you that you've held on to your hurt long enough. I would tell you that your little one would be happy for you. I would tell you to trust me. Starting a family is what we both need. I'm sure of it."

He'd always known when he'd found the right one he would be content to settle down. This conversation, the feelings of hurt and commitment it stirred, had convinced him Natalie was it.

But she simply gazed at him, her sparkling emerald eyes so sad and lost.

He was deciding on his next move when the doorbell rang. He shot a glance in that direction, exhaled then dropped a resigned kiss on her cheek.

"That's Paul. We'll talk more later. We'll talk as much as you like."

She looked as if her heart had been flattened but

finally she nodded and smiled that Mona Lisa smile. "Can I have the keys to your car? I need to go out."

Hesitantly, he fished out his keys.

She was pale, her hands trembling. She wasn't in a state to go anywhere. But he wasn't her keeper, although soon he would be her husband.

Nine

"Are you certain, Natalie? Your hometown doctor could've made a mistake."

Natalie sat in the exquisite sunroom, among the damask cushions and lacy potted ferns, surprisingly calm while Teresa Ramirez tried to rationalise the news she'd just heard.

Natalie had expected this reaction. In fact, when she'd rung Teresa on her cell phone and asked to meet, Natalie had banked on it. News of an otherwise healthy young woman being unable to bear children would likely get the same reaction from anyone.

Denial. Misplaced hope.

Setting down her Waterford cup, Natalie reassured her.

"I had minor surgery two years ago. The specialist explained afterward that I have scars—intrauterine adhesions—from a curettage performed six years ago. It's called Asherman's syndrome. It means I'd have a difficult time conceiving and, if I did conceive, I could very well miscarry again."

Under no circumstances would she risk losing another baby. She'd lived through that cruel, constant pain once. She couldn't live through it again.

"There are other doctors," Teresa said. "Perhaps someone who could help. Alexander's friend…"

But Natalie was shaking her head. It was understandable Teresa would have doubts. She did not.

Teresa studied her for a long moment as if she needed time to absorb the finality of it all. To a woman who looked forward to enjoying many children, of course it would be difficult to digest. Maybe even worrying.

"But you've told Alexander about the pregnancy," Teresa finally said. "About the baby you lost?"

Natalie explained more fully.

"Within twenty-four hours, Alex and I went from a *no-strings-attached love affair* to a shock engagement announcement, to him insisting that I wear his ring. He made it all sound so real. So doable."

A beautiful home and children. A happy life.

Resigned, Natalie slanted her head. "But I know that's impossible. I'd planned to tell him everything after he heard back from Mr. Zhang."

Natalie gave Teresa background on the research project venture and Alex's delicate position with regard to gaining the cautious Mr. Zhang's full commitment.

"But when Alex heard that reporters had been snooping around this morning," Natalie went on, "he said we had to make a stand, make a public statement, because neither of us had anything to hide and—"

She broke off and let out that breath. "I knew it had gotten way out of hand and I had to tell him right away. I got as far as the pregnancy and the birth…"

"He understood?"

Natalie remembered his reaction and smiled.

"He was more understanding than I could ever have dreamed. I could see in his eyes that he hurt for me. Then he spoke about life being empty without children, that I would realise that, too, and be happy when we had our first."

Setting her jaw, Natalie swallowed to control the push of tears. "I wanted to tell him the rest but the words…they stuck in my throat."

He was so passionate and resolute about them being together.

Weary, Natalie sat back. "Then Paul showed up at the house and Alex said we'd talk later."

Teresa set down her cup. "What can I do?"

"This morning Alex said he was committed to making a life for us…for our children. He's so determined, even if I tell him it's impossible, now I'm not sure he'll accept it. Like you, I think he'll try to tell me that something can be done. That some miracle will occur. I don't want to put either of us through that useless kind of hope."

"You want me to talk to him?"

Natalie nodded. She knew Teresa had been surprised by her visit. They'd met only once. She'd come because Teresa was one person Natalie was certain Alex would listen to and today she needed an ally.

"If I need you to help convince him—yes. He needs to let this go. I don't want anyone hurt because of any delusions he might want to hold on to."

Teresa crossed her legs and clasped her hands around a knee. "Be honest. You're also thinking of Bridget Davidson and her baby."

Natalie blinked. "Of course."

"It's not proven that woman is truly carrying Alexander's child."

"You're implying that if Bridget slept with one man, she could've slept with two, three, even four." She'd seen the same accusation in the darting glances at Constance Plains even now when she visited. "If it's proven that Alex isn't the father, he admits that there's at least a possibility that he could be."

"Are you saying he should take responsibility for that child even if the test comes back negative?"

"I'm only saying that I feel for Bridget's situation. It's easy to look from the outside in and say an unplanned pregnancy could've been avoided. That she should've been more careful. But Bridget wasn't alone in creating that baby. And if she turns out to be any type of mother she'll stand by her child no matter who does or does *not* stand by them."

Her gaze imploring, Teresa reached for Natalie's hand. "Please, wait until those results are in."

"It won't make a difference. Yes, I think he should be with Bridget if that baby is his. But if it's proven he's not the father then at least he'll be free to find someone who can give him what he wants."

A family.

"And what if he simply wants you?" Teresa asked. "I've seen the way he looks at you."

"Have you seen the way he looks at that doubloon?"

Teresa seemed to hold her breath before lowering her gaze. She nodded. "I saw the way my father and grandfather looked at it, too. It's always been a foregone conclusion that Alex would one day have at least one son to carry on the legacy. But perhaps you mean more to him than that."

"Men are less complicated than women. He cares for me, I know that. But…"

"But he hasn't said he loves you?"

Holding her gaze Natalie shook her head.

Teresa's lips bowed into a perceptive smile. "You must love him very much."

Her chest squeezed but Natalie squared her shoulders. "I won't let myself."

It would only hurt more to slip any further toward that emotion. She was strong. She would stay strong.

"I wish you would reconsider, but if you won't…" Teresa found and clasped Natalie's hand again. "If you need me, I'll be there."

Half an hour later, Natalie steered Alex's Audi back into the drive. A tall, built man wearing dungarees and a bottle-green T-shirt stood on the wide lush footpath. As she stopped before the opening automatic gates, the man turned his head. His aviator glasses glinted in the sun and a flicker of recognition played around his mouth before he went back to hosing philodendrons.

She shook her brain.

Paul Brennan watering flowers? Talk about undercover.

Cruising up the drive, she half expected to find Alexander waiting on the veranda, but other than Paul keeping guard out front, there wasn't a breath of movement anywhere.

She left the car and entered the house, feeling better for having spoken with Teresa Ramirez. Alexander respected his sister's opinion; he'd said so many times. There was no question Alexander needed to know her secret—that she would never be a mother again—and now she was certain that Teresa would back her position up.

Her admission couldn't wait until Alex heard back from Zhang. What if Zhang asked for more time? What if it dragged out for months? The corporate world was known for delays and in the meantime she would only sink deeper into the mire of intentional omission. Which wasn't so far off deceit.

In the kitchen, she felt the coffeepot. Warm.

After deciding to check out the study next, she confirmed again in her own mind that even if through some miracle she did conceive and go to term, as much as she wanted a baby, as much as she adored Alexander, the fact that he didn't love her, and couldn't seem to see that was a concern, would eat at her and her happiness. When she wasn't able to hide her angst any longer, he would in turn grow upset. Perhaps distant. She wouldn't want a child growing up in that kind of environment.

She darted a look around the cherrywood panels of the study. Not here, either.

Alexander Ramirez was a titan in business but a family man at heart, she decided, heading for the living room. This time next year he would either be married to Bridget Davidson, or dating someone new, as it should be. That didn't mean she regretted having met him, or the amazing time they'd spent together.

As she approached the living room in the northern wing, Natalie heard Alex's voice filter out. She crossed beneath a monstrous ornate arch and saw him sitting in a deep leather armchair, phone pinned to his ear, eyes shut, finger and thumb pinching the bridge of his nose.

Even if they knew each other a hundred years, her feelings would never fade…the skip her heart gave whenever her gaze was drawn to him, the flutter low in her belly whenever she admired the magnificent tone of his body, the regal planes of his face. Even knowing they had to part didn't lessen the knowledge.

He was the man meant for her.

The man she could love with all her heart if only she let herself.

"I think you're making a mistake," Alex said into the mouthpiece, straightening and at the same time spotting her. He motioned her in and, her pulse racing, she inched forward.

"I know all about the economic climate." He nodded at the words spoken on the other end. "I respect that. Sure. That's not in dispute." He grunted. "Fine. I understand. Hopefully we can team up some time in the future."

Disconnecting, he found her gaze and tried for a smile. She wandered over and he pulled her down onto his lap.

"That was Zhang," he said, absently curling hair behind her ear. "He's not going ahead. He's not confident enough in the project."

"Oh, Alex." Biting her lip, she wrapped her arms around his neck as her heart sank for him. "I'm sorry. I feel as if it's my fault."

He unravelled her arms and questioned her eyes. "How do you get that?"

"If we hadn't been going out, if I hadn't gone that night…"

"If the world was painted orange with red stripes." He laughed but the shine had gone from his eyes.

"Do you have time to find someone else?"

"Another entity is ready to go ahead. The research team need funds now." He tossed his phone onto the side table. "Important thing is the work will be done, people will be better off, and I'll live to fight another day." His head rocked back and for a long moment he stared, unseeing, at the high moulded ceilings. "Good thing we're on vacation. God, I need a break."

Her heart went out to him, but while this was a blow, she couldn't let anything stand in the way. It was time for her full admission. *Past* time.

She wet her lips, hauled down a breath.

"Alex, I—"

His jaw firm, he met her gaze. "Please, I don't want to talk about Zhang. What I need now more than anything is you. I look at you and nothing else matters." His earnestness dissolved and he gave into a self-deprecating smile. "I must be getting soft."

Touched, she combed her palm over his jaw. Whatever it was, it only drew her to him all the more.

He was so strong, invincible, and yet at this moment he seemed to need her so much. She couldn't help wanting to hold on to what they had. She wished the world would simply pass them by and it could be like this between them forever.

Vital. Real.

A twinkle returned to his eye. "Do you realise I haven't kissed you in two full hours?"

She grinned. "You've been counting?"

"Every minute."

He brought her mouth to his, kissing her lightly at first, his lips nipping at hers, the tip of his tongue sliding along their join. With his fingers kneading the back of her neck, their emotions swelled. He angled his head and the kiss became a kiss in earnest, penetrating, meaningful. The kind of caress that stole every drop of common sense and set her heart beating wildly in her throat.

When their lips parted, she kept her eyes closed, desperately wanting to pull him back.

Just one moment more. Just one.

He brushed her nose with his. "I have an idea. Actually I had it last night waiting for you."

On a sigh, she drifted back to reality and laid her head on his shoulder. "What's that?"

"Let's escape and get out of Sydney for a while," he said. "I have a place on the Gold Coast. Nothing grand like this, but there's excellent restaurants and shows nearby. It's right on the water on a secluded beach." She felt the rumble in his chest as he groaned. "That's what I need. You and the sound of the waves washing on the shore."

She sat up slowly.

It sounded divine, but also impossible. For two reasons. Reasons that couldn't be ignored.

"Shouldn't you stay here in case—"

"Mateo phoned," he said, anticipating her question. "He has Bridget's sample. We'll know by the end of the week. Early next week at the latest." He held her face and pleaded with his eyes. "We need to think about us, just us alone for a few days. Tomorrow will come soon enough."

Ten

They boarded the aircraft and touched down at Coolangatta Airport at six-fifteen that evening. Natalie knew she dated a man of extraordinary wealth, but a private jet was a luxury she couldn't quite fathom. The wine alone would've cost as much as a week's rent.

Alex's personal assistant organised for the beach house to be serviced and a limousine to collect them at the airport. The car drove to a secluded address where she was immediately hooked by the sound of washing waves and fresh cool scent of salty air. While the driver sorted the luggage, she and Alex wandered through an exotic Bali-style garden, complete with lagoon pool and trickling Buddha waterfall.

The interior was "open plan" at its best and Natalie gasped at the otherworld scene greeting her at the room's far end. As if tugged by an invisible string, she drifted through the spacious entry then living room, over polished dark timber flooring, past the opened concertina doors and out onto a deck that presided over a fairy-tale stretch of sand and, beyond that, endless shadowy sea.

A faint sliver hung high in diamond-flecked sky while torches, blazing around the deck, loaned a mystical contrast to nature's blanket of dark. In the distance, a curlew cried and frogs croaked in the hope of rain.

Natalie hugged herself and sighed.

Paradise.

When Alex suggested coming here, her conscience had said no even as every other instinct had begged her to agree. He'd suffered a blow when Zhang had pulled out of the research venture. Who knew what to expect with the paternity test results? Today he'd needed her and so, for a final time, right or wrong, she'd relented.

When Alex's warm arms wrapped around her from behind, she pushed those thoughts from her mind and leaned back against him.

For long moments they perused the rolling sea.

"Now I know why you couldn't wait to get here," she said.

"It's not a private cove but with the steep headlands on either side I don't see many visitors. It's definitely a different feel to my Vaucluse place."

"Or the Quinton mansion."

His raspy cheek caressed hers. "You approve?"

"You could say that."

"Are you tired?"

She nodded. *Totally bushed.*

He inhaled and his hard chest pressed against her back. "Then I'll control myself and simply hold you tonight."

She rotated in his arms. "Don't be a gentleman for my sake."

Stretching on tiptoe, she kissed him in the flickering torchlight while his earlier words wove along the edges of her mind.

Tomorrow would come soon enough.

Six blissful days later, Natalie lay on a towel on the beach watching Alexander spear through a succession of tumbling turquoise waves. They'd been to the Gold Coast Casino to catch a show, and had eaten at some marvellous restaurants, alfresco as well as fine dining. However, the previous night was their most special and simply because it had been so ordinary. Toasted sandwiches for supper, a movie followed by a warm cosy bath for two, then a night of uninterrupted sleep.

He'd woken her not long after sunrise, tracing his lips down her arm. Stretching, she'd rolled over and brought her naked body flush with his. Their kisses were unhurried yet filled with more passion than she'd ever known. And when his mouth had dropped lower, over her chin, down her throat, she'd wound her arms up over her head and had allowed him every delicious liberty.

She was near senseless by the time they'd joined in earnest, his magnificent body covering hers. He'd searched her eyes as they tried to hold back the tide, tried to make the intensity and wonder last.

Now she shifted onto her side again, this time waving back as Alex strode out of the water. As he sent her a dazzling smile, shaking off his hair and his hands, her chest tightened. "Tomorrow" was here. Alex expected to hear from Mateo today. Being together this way, so carefree and lazy for almost a week, had made the complications surrounding their lives seem like a bad dream.

Alex fell on the towel beside her, his bronzed body glistening with beads of water. She leaned closer, wanting to taste the salt on his bicep but he shook his head a second time, shooting cold spots through the air and over her.

She jackknifed to a sit. "Hey, stop that!"

He stole a quick kiss and spoke against her lips. "Come for a swim."

"I'm enjoying my book," she teased.

He kissed her again, thoroughly this time, his strong cold arm drawing her near, his fresh cool lips fully capturing hers.

The kiss ended in lingering, erotic snatches. His eyes closed, he murmured, "Wouldn't you rather get some exercise?"

"What did you have in mind?"

"You heard me." He tugged at her bikini bottoms. "Getting you wet."

Her body reacted, the cells flashing like tiny meteors through her system. His innate sexual pull never failed to draw her in. But if he meant for them to make love here, now, in the open…

She cast a cautious look around. "You told me this was a public beach."

"With no one around for miles."

In one fluid motion, he rolled her over, pinning her playfully beneath him.

She combed her fingers through his cold damp hair as his sea drops fell upon her arms and her chest. Resisting his charm wasn't normally an option— usually she didn't *want* to resist—but he wasn't winning this one.

"There's a perfectly good bed inside," she murmured, running a fingertip around the shell of his ear.

"I don't know if I can wait that long."

"Then maybe you ought to go for another dip. By the feel, the water's cold."

His beautiful mouth twitched. "If you say so."

It seemed she'd only blinked and he was on his feet, swooping her up over his shoulder like an unsuspecting sack. Next thing her torso was slapping against his back as he marched toward the deep.

As the upside-down waves drew closer, she beat against his hip.

"Don't you dare!"

Chuckling, he continued into the ocean up to his thighs. One moment her hair was dragging in the water, the next he'd swung her around and down onto her feet. She was ready to yelp, but the water wasn't as cold as she'd thought. In fact, it was perfect…refreshing and just cool enough on a warm cloudless day.

He gathered her extra close, his toned abdomen reminding her of ruts of steel, his shoulders magnificent and hard.

"Don't be afraid of sharks." His splayed fingers coursed down her sides. "I'll protect you."

"Who'll protect me from you?"

His hold nudged her hips closer to his. "You don't feel safe?"

Given the size of that erection?

She held on to his pecs, trying to keep her distance

while also desperate to knead all that hot human granite dusted with hair.

"Alex, people don't make love in the open in the middle of the day like this."

He laughed, his sexy eyes saying without words, *So naïve.*

She held her breath.

If she let him kiss her again, she'd be lost. This beach might look deserted but there were eyes everywhere…particularly reporters' eyes. Still, Alex looked so determined, so incredibly strong in will and build, she couldn't think of how to escape.

Unless…

Relaxing against him, she offered her mouth for his to take. When he smiled and she had him off guard, she slipped free and dived away.

She wasn't quick enough. He seized her ankle and effortlessly dragged her back through the water.

Soaking wet, and out of air, she swept back her hair then set her hands on her hips.

He was laughing. "*Carino,* don't run away. If you feel that strongly, I promise to behave."

She narrowed her eyes. "I'm not sure I believe you."

His expression sobered as his hand searched out hers. "You can believe that I respect you."

Emotion flared in her eyes before she smiled softly. "Really?"

"Really."

He wanted her to know that he wouldn't hold her teen pregnancy over her head. It had been a shock, but he'd accepted her past and that was that. Now he was only concerned about the future. Once this paternity issue was settled, they'd set a date and start a family.

Hell, they could start now.

Her smile wavered. "You could almost convince me."

His shoulders rolled back.

She was thinking about what came next. Thinking he might marry Bridget if the test proved positive. Admittedly, if the baby was his, he'd wondered how he'd react the first time he saw his child. Would he feel an immediate bond, a fierce need to protect and possess?

Would it be a boy?

He sucked back a breath.

All that couldn't change how sure he felt about making Natalie his wife. He needed to reassure her… With words, another kiss?

But then the answer seemed obvious.

He gripped her hand and, knees stepping high, ran with her from the water. On the beach, he swooped up the towels and hauled her, laughing, around the side of the house. He flicked a switch and automatic gates shut them in.

As he continued their escape to the secluded front, she sounded out of breath but excited, despite herself.

"Alexander, what are you doing?"

Reaching the waterfall, he finally put on the brakes and turned to face her.

"I plan to worship every inch of you." Holding her shoulders, he pressed a lingering kiss to her brow.

"But—"

He set his finger against her lips. "If you're about to say, *but we're in our own private paradise, where I feel completely secure,*" his mouth lowered to taste to her neck, "then don't let me stop you."

As her head rolled to one side, his hand on her back moved higher to tug her bikini bow free.

Her bunched fingers unfurled on his chest. "You're insatiable," she growled.

"Is that a complaint?"

"It's a fact, and here's another."

She began to lower, first her cool body, followed by her fingers as she sank against him all the way until she was on her knees.

"As far as you're concerned," she murmured against his skin, "I'm insatiable, too."

She released his erection from his shorts then, steadying the beating shaft in her hand, rolled her tongue around the sensitive tip one way, then the other, before taking him into her mouth.

As he hardened more, his eyes drifted shut and Alexander lifted his smiling face to the sun.

When she made love to him, he was everything he could be. Everything and more.

Sizzling attraction, mutual respect, the woman he wanted to bear his children…

Soon he would tell her.

They were the perfect fit.

Together they would make the perfect family.

Eleven

"Maybe we ought to think about moving?"

Alex heard Natalie's suggestion but hesitated answering. An hour had passed since they'd arrived at the pool, and he was more than content to remain with her coiled safely in his arms.

Running a hand over her naked curves, which seemed to grow more voluptuous by the hour, he nipped her earlobe. "I'm happy."

"But aren't you hungry? Men are supposed to have appetites."

"I have appetites. They begin and end with you."

Her laugh was husky, taking him back to the

words and sounds she'd made just moments ago. Unrestrained murmurings and moans that had set his blood alight. Interesting that no matter how many times they made love, those fires were always hungry to be fed.

As he trailed fingertips up and down her back, she sighed and rested her cheek against his shoulder. "It would be easy, wouldn't it, to stay here forever?"

"Why don't we?"

Her head came up and she studied him, half questioning, maybe half believing. But then her emerald eyes dimmed, she untwined from his arms and waded away.

Her ethereal shape ascended the pool steps, dark hair pouring down her back, ripe hips swaying hypnotically, then came the endless magic of her legs.

A goddess, yes. In form, intelligence and spirit. He'd been lucky to find her. And he would keep her at any cost.

While she knotted a towel under her arms, he pushed out the water and dried off.

"I'll get the book you left on the beach," he said, stepping into his trunks. "Do you want to go out for lunch or hunt something down in the kitchen?"

She thought for a moment. "I feel like chicken salad sandwiches with lots of mayo."

He snatched a kiss. "Sounds good."

While she entered the house through a side door,

he opened the gate, moved out onto the beach then stopped dead.

A boy, maybe eight, was excavating a hole not far from where Natalie had lain an hour ago. He had dirty blond hair, was almost too lean, and the enthusiasm he put into the dig was nobody's business.

Recovered from the surprise, Alex moved forward. "Hey, there."

The boy glanced up, wiped his brow with the back of his forearm. "Hey."

His eyes, as blue as today's noonday sky, dropped again and he went back to work.

Alex's mouth swung to one side. He didn't know kids that age could be so focused.

"Are you building a sandcastle?"

The boy kept his eye on his work. "Hunting for treasure."

Crossing his arms, Alex smothered a smile at the same time casting an eye up and down the beach. No parents around. No dog in tow.

Alex stepped closer. "I don't know of any treasure buried around here."

After dropping his spade, the boy pried his battered water bottle off his belt. "A hundred years ago a bunch of robbers buried some stolen jewels somewhere on this beach. I'm gonna find them and get the reward." He chugged back a couple of mouthfuls then swiped the bottle over his brow. "You can help if you want."

Robbers? Stolen jewels? The boy in Alexander couldn't help but be curious.

"How do you know you're digging in the right place?"

The boy wrestled a map from his boardies' back pocket…a torn piece of exercise paper with squiggles drawn in red and blue texter. In the map's centre sat a big black cross.

He tapped the spot as if that symbol verified his claim, then folded the paper and stuffed it away.

"He was a normal, everyday guy," the boy said as he started digging again.

Alex scrubbed his jaw. "Who was?"

"The robber. Then his son got sick. He needed money to buy medicine so he robbed a bank and got to be the toughest gangster around."

Alex smiled.

Good story.

"What will you do with the reward?"

"Buy medicine just like he did."

"Buy medicine for whom?"

"My mum."

"Why does she need medicine?"

"Cancer."

As the boy pointed to his chest, the breath leached from Alex's lungs. He blinked several times then cursed under his breath.

The boy's head slanted. "Whadja say?"

"I said," Alex cleared his throat, "where's your father?"

"Don't have one."

Alex's jaw tightened. Well, that plain sucked. This kid deserved a dad. *Every* child deserved a father.

Feeling as if ants were crawling up his back, Alex shivered then gathered his straying thoughts. "Do you live around here?"

Maybe he was on holiday. There were only half a dozen homes on the stretch leading to this point.

The boy jerked a thumb and glanced over his shoulder. "In the house with the big purple tree out front."

Alex knew it. The place had deteriorated since his last visit.

The boy was studying him as if maybe he shouldn't be saying so much. Smart kid.

Finding his I'm-not-a-bad-guy smile, Alex put out his hand. "I'm Alexander Ramirez."

The boy hesitated then shook. "Fred."

Alex's brows jumped. "Pardon?"

"Fredrick Green, just like grandpa."

"Is your grandfather around?"

"Not for a while."

Alex didn't have the heart to ask about grandma.

Instead he peered into the hole. "So, mind if I dig for a while?"

Fred thrust the plastic blue spade out. "Tell me when you're tired."

Alex dug for maybe ten minutes while Fred gave pointers and chatted about school friends and playing soccer. He offered Alex some water from his bottle several times.

Stretching his back, Alex threw the spade over his shoulder and finally took a swig. "This treasure hunting's hard work. You hungry?"

"Sure."

"You like chicken salad sandwiches?"

Fred slid a look up the sand. "I havta get back to my mum."

"We could do her up a sandwich, too."

"I usually give her vegemite," his thoughtful look dissolved into a gap-toothed smile, "but she likes chicken almost as much."

So much for the beach being deserted.

On her way to the fridge, Natalie had spotted Alex through the kitchen window speaking with a young boy. A handsome young man, with a mop of fair hair and a serious expression. He looked like he needed a good feed.

Leaning forward on the counter, propping her chin in the cup of her hands, she wondered how often she'd seen Alexander wear sharp business suits or tuxedos. But this beachside lifestyle suited him as much, if not more. He looked so at home.

When the boy handed over his toy shovel and Alex began digging, she laughed.

They made quite a team, the billionaire and the boy.

When her heart tugged, she straightened and crossed to her handbag. She found her cell phone and set the specs to camera mode.

Back at the kitchen window, she watched for a while more, just enjoying the scene. She'd lifted the lens at the same time Alex handed back the toy shovel and sauntered toward the house. She hesitated and took the shot anyway. And another. He was so wonderfully masculine, she could imagine herself poring over these shots after…

Emotion jumped in her throat and she set her jaw.

She wouldn't think about that now. She wouldn't let herself get upset. The day had been too perfect.

As he walked in through the opened veranda doors, she slotted the phone away and, reaching for the bread loaf, asked brightly, "Who's your friend?"

"Sure you can handle it?"

She quit dealing bread. "Why? What's wrong?"

"That little boy's Fred Green."

"Cute name."

"Not so cute circumstances. His mother has cancer."

"Oh my…" Her knees suddenly weak, she leaned against the kitchen counter.

A precious daughter had been taken away from this mother, and that boy's mother might be taken away from her son. There was no rhyme or reason to life. Or death.

She held her pitching stomach. "Did he tell you anything else?"

"He likes chicken salad sandwiches," he grinned, "even if his mum prefers vegemite."

She found a soft smile. "Gotta love a patriotic soul." She turned and dealt out four more rounds of bread.

As she dug into the butter dish, he moved to stand beside her and they gazed at Fred, shovelling tirelessly in the sand.

"Does he want to dig his way to China?" she asked.

He told her a story about robbers and jewels and a reward that would buy medicine. By the end, her throat was aching. That little boy didn't know how brave he was.

Setting her mind to the task—Fred must be hungry after all that hard work—she finished the sandwiches, wrapped them in wax paper and placed them in a bag. On an afterthought, she swung a carton of milk out from the fridge.

"A household can never have enough." She plonked both the carton and bag in Alex's arms.

His dark eyes sparkling, Alex brushed his lips against her cheek then went back outside. A moment later, with supplies in hand and shovel pinned to his chest, Fred Green marched off down the beach.

Alex watched for the longest time before he wandered back up the sand. When he saw her at the window, Natalie sniffed back tears and set her mouth into a smile. He signalled—a swerve with his arm, which meant he was tracking around the front for some reason. Perhaps he'd left something by the pool.

Soon after, he entered through the side door, a newspaper under his arm.

"The local rag," he told her, placing it on the table and joining her to inspect how lunch was progressing.

She glanced over her shoulder at the paper and her stomach twinged. After these past few days, she didn't know if she would ever look at a paper the same way. Why had he gone to collect it?

Picking up the bread knife, she tried to sound casual. "What's so important in today's news?"

"Apparently Fred had his picture taken with his soccer team."

Almost sighing her relief, she finished cutting sandwich triangles with vigour. "I want to see, too."

She set their plates on the table while Alex washed his hands, his air noticeably pensive.

"Doesn't it make you wonder what happens to kids like that?"

Did it ever.

Ann Templar was a Constance Plains single mother who, at only twenty-eight, dropped dead on her morning run. Her twin girls, which were in Natalie's third grade class, disappeared off the face of the planet. No one talked about it and Natalie had been too scared to ask.

"Hopefully his mother will be okay." Natalie prayed she would be.

That didn't satisfy him.

"I mean, do they get shoved in an orphanage, or thrown at a run of foster homes?" Grunting, he wiped his hands on a towel. "Fred could kiss any soccer career goodbye."

Already seated, Natalie reached for the paper but hesitated. She almost didn't want to say it.

"Where's his dad?"

Joining her, he snatched out his chair. "In hell, for all I care."

Natalie could only look at him. He was thinking of himself. Of his own responsibility to Bridget. How he'd need to be there, commit his all, if that baby was his. She understood. She supported him. And at some stage she'd get over him.

Or that's what she had to tell herself.

He bit into the sandwich, told her it was good, then unrolled and scanned the paper's back page. "Seems lots of kittens are needing homes around here."

"I like cats."

He grinned, flipped the paper over, turned a page and another. She'd taken a bite when, out the corner of her eye, she saw his tanned hand clench over the print.

She slid a glance at the headline and the bread she swallowed stuck in her throat.

No Family For Ramirez Tycoon. Bride-To-Be Barren.

Her heartbeat booming high in her chest, she ventured a look at his face.

An icy calm seemed to have settled over him. She'd never seen his eyes appear harder, almost unseeing.

He calmly set the paper aside.

Natalie swallowed again. She'd hoped for a better way, a kinder time, to bring this out, but at least now they couldn't hide from the truth any longer.

The moment had come.

"Aren't you going to say something?" she ventured.

"Something like, I want to kill those SOBs? I'll have them retract it," his fingers closed around his glass of juice, "then I'll sue their ass."

Her stomach sank lower. When this was over she would cry as she'd never cried before. Then, she suspected, she would never cry again. Half wishing for that kind of all consuming numbness now, she inhaled a steadying breath.

"Alex, it's true."

He set his glass down. "What's true?"

"I can't have children."

He slanted his head at her and his mouth hooked into a patient smile. "That's ridiculous. You had a child. You'll have another, and with me."

He reached for her hand but she slid it away.

She guessed the reporter had gotten his facts right. But from where? Ill-gotten medical files? Certainly not from Teresa. Obviously a city paper had broken the news. Heck, the Plains Post would have those words blazoned on its front page. She could almost hear the sanctimonious chorus of *oohs* and *ahhs* from here.

"I have a...condition," she forced herself to say. "I wanted to tell you. I tried..."

His expression changed, half admiration, half irritation.

"*Carino,* I'm no fool. You're saying this in the hope that I'll marry Bridget. I understand how you feel. I agree. That baby should have a father. If I'm responsible I'll be the best dad I can be."

"Whether or not you marry Bridget won't change the fact that we can never have a family of our own."

His eyes narrowed and brow pinched. His gaze held hers for a long tense moment before he growled, "My God, you're serious."

Hating his expression—disbelief, horror, suppressed rage—she nodded slowly. "I'm afraid so."

On a burst of energy, he thrust up to his feet. Natalie gasped as his chair skated across the timber and hit a hutch.

"Mateo's an expert," he ground out. "I'll call him now."

He moved to stride off, but she caught his corded arm. There was one last admission to make.

"There is a procedure, some chance I could conceive. But there's also a chance I'll miscarry again and again." Her throat closed unbearably tight. "I can't do that, Alex. I can't lose another baby." Her voice broke. "It would kill me."

His shoulders slowly dropped and his dark, usually clear gaze took on a haunted look. "Mateo will have some solution. Bed rest. Medications…"

But she shook her head. "When we first began dating I had no idea our relationship would go this far this quickly. I didn't think for a minute you would feel so strongly."

He pulled her up and held both her wrists against his beating chest. "To hell with *feel strongly*. We're meant to be together."

Her insides gripped and she swallowed down a sob. "You're not listening." She'd known he wouldn't. He'd made a decision about her, the wrong decision, and he didn't want to be proven wrong. "I spoke to Teresa—"

His expression soured. "Teresa knew about this and I didn't?"

"She supports me. You mightn't think it now, but it's best we accept this and move on."

She wanted to give him that son. She wished that he loved her, as much as she loved—

A crippling ache pushed up her throat. She pressed her lips together and swallowed back the tears.

The fact that she had fallen in love with him was perhaps worse than anything. After these days alone together, when the outside world had left them alone, it had seemed unimaginable they should part. And yet there was no alternative. There was no answer to their problem. No remedy but goodbye.

He dropped her hands then turned a tight circle, like a big cat caught in a cage.

When he stopped, his gaze pierced hers. His voice was rough, almost accusing. "You should have told me."

When the situation had reached a certain level, yes, she should have.

But, "I didn't put this in motion. You did, by telling the reporter we were engaged. I told you no then, so many times, but you kept pushing."

"You can't tell me you don't want what I want."

"I do." She wanted to marry him, have his children. Have the successful life she'd once dreamed of.

"When I marry, Alex…I want to marry for love."

His jaw clenched as his dark eyes glistened. "Seems we don't always get what we want."

Fighting the urge to do the unthinkable, break down and cry, she lifted up her chin.

"You said you respected me." *Please, Alexander.* "Respect me now."

"You won't reconsider?"

"I can't."

The attention she'd thought she'd seen softening his eyes earlier hardened now to black ice. His magnificent chest rose and fell several times before he nodded once and strode away.

"Pack your things," he said over his shoulder and she thought she heard his voice crack. "Pack them now. It's best we leave straight away."

Twelve

On entering the study, Alexander shut the door, paced the room then sank into the couch and dropped his head in his hands.

Then he swallowed.

Hard.

The tragic part was that he understood Natalie's dilemma, or as much as he was able. To bury a child would be a horror that would play on her mind till the end of time. He'd been committed to her recovery. Building a family of their own seemed the very best plan.

He closed his eyes and pressed the heels of hands against his eyes.

How could he have known about her condition? She hadn't given it a name, only that she was unlikely to conceive, and if she did fall pregnant she could lose the child she carried. Natalie had said she couldn't live through that again.

But the fighter in him said they should try. He had a sixth sense for success and he knew in his heart they could succeed in this. They didn't need to have a dozen children. Not even three. If they could have only one child together and then...

His gut twisted and he pushed to his feet.

God, he'd never felt more powerless. Alexander Ramirez, wunderkind venture capitalist. The shining pinnacle of a long line of men who knew what it meant to win. What it meant to influence while deflecting influence from himself.

How in the name of heaven had his no-strings lover come to mean so much? Natalie said she wouldn't marry without love. He couldn't consider it. He'd made a conscious choice not to leave himself that exposed to anyone. Taking a wife and having a family was one thing, but love for a woman could turn a man's mind to mush. There were enough men like Raymond Chump around to prove it. A few days completely alone with a beautiful woman couldn't change that truth. Particularly given that Natalie was turning out to be everything he'd planned to avoid. She'd left him no room to move.

His stinging gaze darted and honed in on the desk. He crossed over and threw open the bottom drawer. He found his wallet and, in a special compartment, the Ramirez doubloon.

Since his twenty-first birthday he'd kept this piece in a safe. These last few days, however, he carried the coin with him, perhaps hoping that his ancestors would spirit him an answer to his problem, a problem that had grown to unexpected proportions.

He held the uneven lump of gold, felt its weight as well as its purpose, and more than ever he wanted to remain true to the legend. He wanted this treasure to go to its rightful heir. And if that heir proved to be Bridget Davidson's baby…?

A loud knocking sent his heart catapulting to his throat. Blowing out a breath, he collected himself and went to open the door. Natalie stood before him, her face white as sea salt.

"I'm packed," she told him. "You said we were leaving immediately."

With those few words, all that pent up energy seemed to drain away, and he dropped his gaze from hers. If there was an answer, for the life of him he couldn't see it. He only knew he wanted to take her in his arms and tell her they could work it out. He'd said they'd belonged with each other, yet everything he'd ever believed in shouted for him to walk away.

Surely when they were apart he'd be able to think more clearly. More like his old self.

"I'll get my things together," he said. "Get the driver out."

"How long do you think before we land in Sydney?"

Bemused, he raised his brows. "You're in a rush."

"I need to get back, Alex."

Frowning, he judged her expression more closely. She wasn't merely pale. She looked ready to crumple.

"What's wrong?"

She seemed eager to let him know. "My mother's in the hospital. Mrs. Heigle rang to tell me."

He rushed a hand through his hair. He had no idea who Mrs. Heigle was and he didn't care. How many more blows did they need this week?

"Was she in an accident?"

"It's her heart. Apparently she needs a stint to open up a blocked artery." Her shoulders went back. "I need to be with her."

"And you think driving four hours from Sydney to Constance Plains in your condition is a good idea?" She was trembling.

"I need to be with her." She enunciated each word. "She'd do the same for me."

Alexander exhaled.

Of course she would. Any parent would.

He returned to his desk, grabbed the receiver and called his PA. Madison picked up on the second ring.

"Can you organise to have the jet ready to depart within an hour? Destination?" He looked at Natalie. "Constance Plains."

Three hours later they arrived in Natalie's hometown and Alexander was worried.

Natalie had barely said a word the entire flight. She'd even declined to speak with Teresa when he'd called his sister and Teresa had asked after her. Now, unfastening her belt, Natalie seemed all the more withdrawn, uncommonly pale. The energy that normally radiated from her had vanished.

Was it because she'd given up hope or he had?

But he was all out of ideas. He couldn't marry her. There was no point debating the question of *love*. What good would it do to think about that now? The point was he refused to consider trying to have a family. And if Bridget's baby turned out to be his…

Madison had organized for a rental vehicle, a sedan, in this town, not a limousine. The hospital was typical country fare, wide verandas, a coral tree in the front, looking robust despite the lack of rain. Inside the smell of antiseptic lingered in the air and there wasn't a soul around. As he and Natalie walked the worn linoleum to the tidy reception area, a passing nurse, about Natalie's age, took a double take.

"Tallie?"

Natalie summoned a smile. "How are you, Miriam?"

"I'm fine." She nodded to Alex then gestured down a hall. "Your mum's this way, in a private room." They headed down the corridor. "She had a scare but she's in a stable condition. There's no need for anyone to worry." They stopped before a closed door. "If you need anything, press the buzzer."

"I will. Thanks."

The nurse squeezed Natalie's shoulder, nodded to Alex again, and bustled away.

Alex raised his brows. "This *is* a small town."

Natalie shrugged. "Miriam and I went to school together."

"Have you kept in touch?"

"Besides my mother, I don't keep in touch with anyone from here." She rubbed her arms as though she were cold, or irritated. "I'd like to see her alone, if that's okay."

He stepped back. "I'll wait out here."

After she shut the door behind her, Alex surveyed the area. He could shake down a coffee, check his e-mails. Drive himself crazy wondering how this day would end.

A voice at his back took Alex by surprise.

"You look a little lost."

Alex spun around. A man wearing an out-of-place fedora and classic white coat smiled at him. His hair was white, too, and his pale blue eyes seemed to hold more knowledge than Alex could ever hope to accrue.

Alex smiled, shrugged. "You could say that."

The man put out his hand. "I'm Doctor Hargons."

"Alexander Ramirez."

"I know." His grin was wry as they shook. "I'm afraid the town is abuzz with news about you and Tallie."

Alex frowned. That was the second time he'd heard that nickname.

The doctor tipped his head. "The waiting lounge is this way." They began to walk. "It's a pity that along with fame comes lack of privacy. Some of today's reporters should be thrown in jail."

Alex grinned. "My thought exactly."

They strolled for a while, Dr. Hargons concentrating on the step of his well-loved hushpuppies. "You were aware of Tallie's condition before today's report?"

"Not a clue."

The doctor didn't seem at all surprised. Perhaps he knew more than he was saying.

Alex stopped. "How long have you worked in this hospital?"

"Forty odd years."

"Then you were Natalie's doctor when she delivered?"

"I was also the one who told her the tragic news."

Alex nodded. "As well as the fact she could have problems in the future?"

Doctor Hargons seemed to evaluate Alex for a long moment before he continued.

"A month after the miscarriage, Natalie's mother brought her in. She was running a high temp. I performed an examination. Scarring of the uterus can spread and thicken, which can be a big issue for fertility. There's surgery available, but statistics say twenty to thirty percent of women may remain either unable to conceive or incapable of carrying to term."

"But there is a chance Natalie could fall pregnant. A baby could make it through."

"There is that chance, yes. But there's another consideration just as powerful as physical setbacks." They continued on toward the waiting lounge. "That tiny baby didn't have a chance of pulling through. Naturally Tallie was devastated. She blames herself. Fear of similar complications can be overwhelming for women who miscarry."

They arrived at the lounge and the doctor slid his hands into his coat pockets. "With the baby being over twenty weeks she was named and a funeral took place. Natalie's ritual of visiting the grave every month is well-known here. If her dedication there is anything to go by, she would've made a wonderful mother."

"I'm sure she would have." And still could be.

Movement up the hall caught Alex's eye. Natalie

had left her mother's room and was looking straight at him.

Alex squared his shoulders and shook the doctor's hand again. "Thanks for being so candid."

"I hope it helps. Tallie's a sweet girl. She deserves a happy ending."

A few long strides and Alex was again by Natalie's side. "How's your mother?"

"Sleeping now. But I want to stay a while."

"I'll stay, too."

"You don't have to."

"Nevertheless…" He shot a glance around. "Want to try the hospital coffee? Maybe there's a café nearby. We haven't eaten since breakfast."

Lacing her hands before her, she lowered her gaze, but then met his eyes square on. She looked beyond spent, ready to crumple. Whatever she was about to say, she only wanted to say it once.

"Alex, I appreciate all you've done," she began, "But…I'm sorry. I'd rather that you left now."

He felt the blow like a slug to the chest. And yet when all was said and done, he *should* go. He should get out now and leave Tallie Wilder to her town and to her business. He'd thought they'd belonged together. Some infuriatingly persistent part of him was still twisting his arm. But his more rational side said to get moving. There was nothing left to say.

Taking with him one last memory of her face, her

hair, her scent, he straightened his shoulders and strode for the exit without looking back. He felt winded now but that would pass. He'd thought he'd had his future mapped out with Natalie. He'd been wrong. He could admit it. He'd never been more wrong in his life.

He burst into the fresh air, made it down to the path and was striding past that tree when his cell phone sounded. He wanted to ignore it. Finding a pub with an understanding barman before flying the hell home sounded like a good idea. But the buzz continued until it hit him who might be calling.

After whipping the phone off his belt, he scrutinized the ID, blew out a ragged breath and thumbed the answer key.

Mateo's greeting was all business. "I have the results, my friend. Are you sitting down?"

Alex groaned. Should he curse or look on the bright side? Sounded as if he was going to be a father. He was going to have that heir. An illegitimate heir the way things stood. But if he married Bridget, wouldn't he have a more than acceptable wife, the child that he wanted? And if he was a boy—

Holding his damp forehead. Alex withered onto a nearby bench. "It's positive?"

"No. You're in the clear."

Alex's hand dropped to his lap at the same time the afternoon sun slid out from behind a cloud.

"What did you say?" Alex knew what he'd heard, but he wanted to hear it again.

"The test was negative." There were a few beats of silence. "Alex, are you there?"

"I'm here." And free! Free of paternity tests. Free to never make the same mistake twice, and that went double for falling in love.

He stopped breathing, cocked his head and blinked several times into space.

"Alex? Alexander. Say something."

He shook his head, trying to set his thoughts straight. "Mateo, I don't know if it's the western sun or no food in my stomach or the fact that I'm just getting older." And wiser? The stark, blinding truth had slipped in the back door. He hadn't invited it. He thought he'd outrun it. Yet now it had arrived, he couldn't deny it.

He was about to explain all to Mateo when a familiar sight appeared around the corner. Alex laughed out loud and flagged the driver down.

Two hours later, Natalie walked down the hospital stairs feeling better about her mother's condition, but horrible about the way she'd closed the door on Alex earlier. Though his expression hadn't changed, she'd seen his eyes flare when he'd accepted her dismissal and had bowed off. She believed a part of him was relieved.

She'd felt ill all the flight here. She'd needed time to sit by her mother's bedside without worrying that Alex was waiting outside, talking to well-meaning doctors. No good could come of whispered conversations. Her mind was made and she didn't care what anyone thought of her, or of her stand.

She wished Alex could walk in her shoes for a day. She wasn't being stubborn, merely responsible. She didn't want them both to struggle through another ordeal like the one she'd suffered. When he found happiness with another woman, when he started to build that family, he would thank her for sticking to her guns. He might even find love.

A whirlpool of dry leaves whipped around her shoes as she turned off Reliance Street, ducked into Toys'n'Dolls to make her regular purchase and then headed down Main, the same street she walked the first Monday of every month.

As usual, people with nothing better to do peered out store windows. Old Mrs. Prindle, Natalie was sure, reserved that same bench outside the municipal library every day so as not to miss any action. Their glares burned her back. She didn't care. Blessed numbness was returning. It was so much better than feeling her heart continually knot and sink in her chest.

Anything was better than that.

She heard the purr of the prestige engine before the Bentley appeared on the road beside her.

Her jaw dropped and step faltered while Mrs. Prindle up ahead rose to her feet. The elderly woman and her cane fell back into the bench when Alexander, appearing like a modern day knight, swept out from the Bentley's backseat.

Natalie could barely speak, she was so surprised. "But how…?"

"Paul drove in from Sydney," Alex said, coming to stand before her. "He thought we might need a way to get about."

Natalie shot a glance around Alex's broad frame. In the driver's seat, Paul eased down his sunglasses and winked.

Alex found her elbow and they began to walk. Natalie felt too shell-shocked to object.

"Can I drive you anywhere?" he asked.

"I'd rather walk."

She always walked. It was a ritual. A penance.

"Then I'll walk, too."

No one, not even her mother, came with her on these visits. For six years, she'd clung to tradition, hoping each step might bring her closer to finding some sort of peace. She'd never considered sharing this time. It was too private. Too painful. Now Natalie stopped, assessed his dark gaze, acknowledged the tug of war pulling inside of her, then hesitantly fell back into step.

After a few minutes of walking in silence together, feeling the town's eyes riveted on each step, he spoke.

"I've heard from Mateo."

A shudder sped up her spine. She hugged the stuffed toy to her chest, filled her lungs and offered a thin smile. "Good news?"

His gaze was direct and unreadable. "Natalie, the test was negative."

The air in her lungs left in a whoosh. Weak at the knees, she slumped, and he caught and held her up.

This was good news for Alexander. He wasn't the father of Bridget's baby. He had no obligation to fill. He was free to find himself the perfect bride. Have that perfect family. The family she longed for, too, but would never have.

Natalie gathered herself.

That kind of self-pity would get her nowhere. What about Bridget? She'd been in a similar position once. Single and pregnant. So worried about the future.

"Then who *is* the father?" she asked, straightening and instantly missing the strength and comfort of his arms.

"Mateo passed the results on to Bridget first," Alex explained, beginning to walk again. "He suggested I phone her. She apologised and admitted she knew who the father must be. A musician who her father disapproves of even more than me, which is why she'd broken off their affair. But after Joe took matters into his own hands and gatecrashed Teresa's party, Bridget got in touch with her musician. She told him about the tests, about me." Alex's hands found his trouser pockets. "Seems he confessed his love and said he wanted to marry her either way. He was with her when Mateo rang through the results." Alex gave a grudging smile. "The guy's apparently ecstatic, and so, it would appear, is Bridget."

"I'm glad it worked out for her."

And despite her heart contracting till it hurt, despite knowing this news made no difference to *them,* she was glad the paternity issue had worked out for Alexander, too.

A few minutes later, they entered through the opened cemetery gates. Alex's expression didn't waver as they passed beautifully kept gardens of roses and ferns, among which displayed plaques in memory of so many loved ones. They followed the long winding path that led to the poinciana tree that had begun to bloom red. Then came the hardest moment as well as one she treasured most.

Her wishing time.

Kneeling before a statue of an infant angel, Natalie collected the last toy she'd left behind. Then she set a kiss on the new bear's crown and placed it at the angel's feet.

She was lost in her thoughts—remembering that

tiny hand, the joy at having known her baby for even a short time—when Alex knelt beside her. She hadn't noticed that he'd brought anything along and yet now he stretched to place something between the bear and the heart it held. She caught a flash of old gold and her own heart stopped beating.

The doubloon?

She caught his hand as it withdrew. "What are you doing?"

He turned his hand over and held hers firmly.

"This baby didn't know her father." He searched the depth of her eyes and murmured, "I'd like to be her father now."

It took two beats for the enormity of his act to hit and in that instant she saw in his eyes that he didn't see this as giving up a legacy. It wasn't a sacrifice. It was an act of deeply felt kindness and support. Today he'd given her a gift more precious than he could ever imagine.

He's also given up what was most precious to him. Not just the Ramirez doubloon, but also the pledge that had gone with it, the pledge to continue the name. Instead, by this act, he'd given his pledge to her. A pledge of honor and support. But what could she give him in return? She had nothing.

She gulped down a breath at the same time something raw and starving tore open inside her. Emotion pushed up, burst free and she broke down, her body shaking with quiet sobs as Alexander gathered and held her close.

"I'm sorry for acting the way I did at the beach house," he said against her hair, rubbing her back. "I couldn't see a solution and yet now I see the answer staring me in the face."

Her cheeks hot and wet, she shook her head against his shirt. "I can't let you throw away your future, your life."

He tipped her chin up. His expression was steely except for the gentle gleam in his eyes.

"But that's the answer. My life is empty unless you're in it. I love you, Natalie. I love you whether we have ten children or none." His head slanted. "I only hope you feel the same way."

Her first instinct was to throw herself at him, tell him that she loved him, too. Had perhaps fallen in love with him the moment that they'd met. These past months, like the last six years, she'd tried to subdue and conquer her feelings. Now it felt good to finally, truly admit them, at least to herself. Because she couldn't say those words aloud. Nothing changed the facts.

She wound away from him and pushed to her feet. "You'll find someone else."

Someone of his class, a woman who could be a true wife to him.

He stood, too, then smiled into her eyes for a long, tender moment.

"I don't want anyone else. As sure as we're standing here, I'll never love anyone but you."

"But I can't give you a son. You need an heir. You want a family, children—"

"Weren't you listening?" His eyes were dancing now. "I *love* you."

Her heart tore open and she choked out the words, the horrible, inevitable truth. "I don't know I deserve you."

The smile fell from his face and the emotion in his gaze intensified.

"Forgive yourself, Tallie." His hands found her shoulders and gently winged them in. "Give yourself permission to love again. We belong together, remember?"

Another hot tear sped down her cheek. She was frightened. Happy.

Loved?

She thought of her angel. His doubloon.

We belong together.

Her voice was threadbare. "You really believe that?"

The corners of his eyes crinkled. "Let me show you how much."

He kissed her, like he'd kissed her a thousand times before. Sincerely, deeply. And yet as he held her near, she felt a different emotion ribboning around them, glittering and colourful, joining them as they'd never been joined before.

When he broke the kiss, she felt somehow reborn. Alive as she'd never been before.

He touched his forehead to hers. "Can you live without this every day of your life, because I can't?"

Her lips trembled into a smile. "You can't?"

He gave her that look. *So naïve.*

"Say it, Natalie. Say it and then we can go forward and start to build our life together."

"I love you," she said.

The words came so easily and the world didn't end. She took a breath and said it again. "I love you. I can't help it. I do." She cupped his jaw. "I love you, Alexander. I love you with all my heart."

When he kissed her again, Natalie imagined she heard the whisper of beating wings. Perhaps it was a fruit-dove on its way home to nest, but as she embraced her future husband beneath that glorious sprawling tree, Tallie liked to think it was an angel, sending her wishes, giving her blessing.

Epilogue

Seven months later.

On a sigh, Natalie reclined back in her chair, more than content to watch her husband and Fred Green kick their ball around on the sand. She and Alexander had been at the beach house a full month now and, given her condition, soaking up morning sunshine on this veranda was her favourite thing.

Glancing down, she shaped a palm over her stomach and a wonderfully warm feeling filtered through her.

"I can't believe I have such a lovely big belly."

Mateo, their guest for the weekend, set his iced tea on the table. "Pregnancy suits you. You're both healthy and it shows. Alex's told me many times how you glow."

"Because I've never been happier."

Every woman should know such contentment… an attentive handsome husband and a beautiful baby on the way, thanks to their first explosive time together when she and Alexander hadn't used protection. Given her condition, the chances of conception had been way less than favourable. Her period had been unpredictable and light for six years. She hadn't thought any more about that night until she'd stepped on some bathroom scales and realised the weight she'd gained.

Her hand shaped over her belly again and her brow pinched. "Do you think it'll be a boy?"

Neither she nor Alex had wanted to know beforehand. She would be overjoyed either way, as long as the baby was healthy.

She closed her eyes and prayed.

Please, let my baby be healthy.

"Alexander will be ecstatic whether you give him a son *or* a daughter," Mateo said. "His biggest joy comes from sharing his life with you."

Not so long ago Natalie had believed she would never know motherhood again. She'd been too afraid to even try. But when she'd learned they were pregnant, she'd found a higher level of faith. This new life deserved every ounce of support, belief and love she could muster.

The sixteen week mark had gone by, then twenty, and thirty. In the meantime Bridget had given birth to a gorgeous baby girl. She'd sent a photo. Natalie had been both wistful and pleased for Bridget and her husband. She'd been overjoyed when, a couple of days ago, she and Alex had toasted with chocolate milk reaching their thirty-eighth week.

They seemed to have beaten the odds.

Alexander's hearty chuckle, drifting up from the beach, drew her attention. He'd raced up to Fred and had placed a hand on the youngster's shoulder, commending him on a great shot. Fred head-butted the ball and raced toward the veranda after it while Alex strode up behind, looking delectable in his swim shorts and unbuttoned short-sleeved shirt. The effortless animalistic grace with which he moved left Natalie near breathless with desire—even when she felt ready to pop!

Fred leapt up the veranda steps. "Did you see that last shot, Mrs. Ramirez?"

Laughing, she leaned forward to accept Fred's kiss on her cheek. "I certainly did."

Mateo ruffled Fred's hair. "The Socceroos won't be able to sign you up quick enough."

Fred's eyes lit at the idea of playing for the Australia's international soccer team. With his fledgling talent, and Alex's support, his dream just might come true. Her husband had a way of making the most incredible things happen.

Alexander dug a note out from his wallet and handed the bill to Fred. "I hear the ice cream truck. He doesn't get out here often. Buy some for your mother, too. She likes Turkish Delight."

When she and Alexander had committed to each other seven months ago, Alex had returned to find Fred. He'd offered to pay for Mrs. Green's breast cancer treatment and the best of care. At one point the doctors weren't certain that she'd make it.

Alex had spoken with Natalie about the possibility of adopting Fred should worse come to worst. She'd hugged him tight and agreed without a second thought. Thankfully Fred's mother had made it through and was growing stronger every day.

As Fred sped off, Alex sank down in a chair between his wife and best friend.

Was it possible to fall in love your husband a little more each day? Natalie wondered. He seemed to grow more handsome, more capable, more trusting and giving with every passing hour. When he held her in his arms at night, lately spoon style, an indescribable sense of destiny seemed to settle over her, the way it had that day in the foyer of the mansion.

Theirs was a once-in-a-lifetime type love, the

kind of bond nothing would break and time would only deepen.

"Have you heard from the O'Reileys?" Alex asked, reaching for the pitcher of tea, and Natalie was brought back. They'd had the mansion on the market a week and already a party was interested.

There was, however, a hitch.

"They want us to drop the price."

She named the figure as Alex crossed an ankle over the opposite knee.

"Do it."

"That's a big drop," Mateo said while Natalie could only blink.

"Are you sure?"

He'd changed from the man who'd been driven to succeed at almost any cost into someone who saw the world for what it was…a miracle to be enjoyed and treasured with every breath. No denying money made life easier but it truly couldn't buy happiness. Being content with yourself then sharing your love and good fortune with others did that. Whenever mother-to-be Teresa or May Wilder, fully recovered now, came to visit, that truth was brought home tenfold.

Gazing out over the sparkling lace-fringed waves, Alex thatched his hands behind his head. "You're happy living here, aren't you?"

Her hand dropped upon his hard thigh as she sighed. "Completely."

"I don't need a big-city office." He reached for her hand. "I don't need anything but you."

As if in protest, her tummy gave an almighty kick then an impatient twist up under the right side of her rib cage. Her hold on his leg tightened as she winced.

Alex sat forward. "Are you all right, *carino*?"

"The baby's been moving so much—"

Another kick, this one a doozey and accompanied by a python-like tightening lower down. A damp breaking out on her brow, Natalie tried to regain her breath. She hadn't wanted to bother anyone, she was ten days from her due date, but now she was worried.

Mateo pushed to his feet. "How far apart are the contractions?"

She'd had niggles since dawn but nothing really regular until the last couple of hours.

"I think fifteen minutes. Maybe less. I thought they were Braxton Hicks…rehearsal contractions."

She paused to concentrate as something different seemed to happen inside. Her eyes widened with understanding at the same instant she felt an internal *click*. A moment later, the deck floor was wet beneath her.

Alex leapt up, the surprise in his expression immediately strengthening to confident pride. He bowed over, cupped her face and spoke with affection and commitment lighting his smiling eyes.

"I don't think this is a rehearsal."

Her return smile was robbed by another contraction, this one so fierce, its radiating pain made her feel nauseous. Tipping forward, she groaned in a voice she didn't recognise as a heavy pressure bore down.

Mateo found Alex's arm.

"I'll examine her. We can deliver here if necessary."

As the rolling pain eased, she swallowed and collected herself. "I'm sure we have plenty of time. My bag's packed." She breathed in, out. "I just need to wash my hair."

Mateo merely smiled. "Women and their hair."

As Alex helped her up from her chair, another contraction pushed down and around the baby. Pressing her lips together, she couldn't keep a long guttural groan from escaping. At the instant her legs buckled, Alex caught her and swept her up into his arms.

"To the bedroom." Mateo headed inside, Alex close behind.

"What do you need?"

"My bag from the car. Towels."

In the shuttered cool bedroom, Mateo threw off the quilt and Alex laid her on the sheet with such care she might have been layers of priceless silk. With his head near hers, she filed her fingers through his strong black hair and assured him as well as herself.

"I feel good." *Don't worry.*

Moisture glistened in his eyes. "You've never looked more beautiful."

"Alex," Mateo interrupted, crossing to the attached bathroom, "my bag and towels, please. And call the hospital. Let them know we'll be in some-time today."

Remarkably Alex's hands didn't shake as he collected Mateo's bag then went to gather a pile of towels from the linen press. He strode with full arms back to the room and set his offerings at the end of the bed. Then he rounded the mattress and kissed the palm of his wife's hand. In between contractions now, her sable hair a dark halo around her head, she looked serene.

He kissed her palm again, went to leave to call the hospital, but she gripped his hand.

A delicate pulse beat at the base of her throat as an emotion he couldn't quite grasp flickered in her eyes.

Fear or faith?

"I love you, Alexander. With all my heart."

Emotion prickled behind his nose, his eyes, as he murmured in a thick gravelled voice, "You are my life."

My love.

Then he inhaled. Stepped back. There would plenty of time for this. The rest of their lives. There was nothing to worry about.

In the living room, he called the hospital, explained the situation, then double-timed it back but stopped short of entering the bedroom. The door was shut, which meant…what?

Perhaps he ought to give Natalie some privacy with Mateo. He trusted Mateo beyond any person, doctor or friend. He needed to trust him now with the two persons he prized most in this world.

His wife. His child.

As the minutes ticked by, Alex paced the floor, ploughing a crazed hand through his hair now and then. There'd been Mateo's gentle murmurings, Natalie's groans, finally a baby's sharp cry and then…

Nothing.

For so long now it had been quiet. Worryingly quiet. So quiet he wanted to bang down that door and—

From behind that closed door, he heard his wife cry out, a small hitched sob and his heart fell to the floor. His throat convulsed as suffocating emotion swelled.

Mateo had assured him…

Dammit, he'd said not to worry!

He forced one foot in front of the other, his stomach clenching with each step, his chest rising and falling on ragged breaths. He reached for the handle at the same time the door swung back.

Mateo stood before him. As he removed the surgical gloves, he tipped his head over his shoulder.

Propped up on a soft bank of pillows, Natalie gazed down at the wrapped bundle she held, every line of her body exuding sublime adoration, her flushed cheeks wet with thankful tears. Then she let out another little sob.

A cry of joy.

Alex's shoulder fell against the doorjamb at the same time his own laugh slipped out. Natalie's emerald eyes flicked over. Her face glowing with unsurpassed love, she held out her hand...the hand that bore his wedding band.

Feeling both weak yet immeasurably strong, Alex moved forward but then looked to Mateo.

"Yes, come in, my friend." Beaming, Mateo stepped aside. "Meet your new baby son."

* * * * *

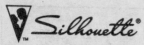

REQUEST YOUR FREE BOOKS!

2 FREE NOVELS PLUS 2 FREE GIFTS!

Passionate, Powerful, Provocative!

COMING NEXT MONTH
Available October 13, 2009

#1969 MILLIONAIRE IN COMMAND—Catherine Mann
Man of the Month
This air force captain gets a welcome-home surprise: a pretty
stranger caring for a baby with an unquestionable family
resemblance—to him! Yet once they marry to secure the child's
future, will he want to let his new wife leave his bed?

#1970 THE OILMAN'S BABY BARGAIN—Michelle Celmer
Texas Cattleman's Club: Maverick County Millionaires
Falling for the sexy heiress was unexpected—but not as
unexpected as her pregnancy! Though the marriage would be for
business, their bedroom deals soon became purely pleasure.

#1971 CLAIMING KING'S BABY—Maureen Child
Kings of California
Their differences over children—she wanted them, he didn't—had
this couple on the brink of divorce. Now his wife has come back
to his ranch…with their infant son.

**#1972 THE BILLIONAIRE'S UNEXPECTED HEIR—
Kathie DeNosky**
The Illegitimate Heirs
The terms of his inheritance bring this sexy playboy attorney a
whole new set of responsibilities…including fatherhood!

#1973 BEDDING THE SECRET HEIRESS—Emilie Rose
The Hightower Affairs
When he hires an heiress as his private pilot, he's determined
to find proof she's after a friend's family money. Each suspects
the other of having ulterior motives, though neither expected the
sparks that fly between them at thirty thousand feet!

#1974 HIS VIENNA CHRISTMAS BRIDE—Jan Colley
Posing as the fiancé of his brother's P.A., the playboy financier is
happy to reap the benefits between the sheets…until secrets and a
family feud threaten everyone's plans.

SDCNMBPA0909

sort of engaged. Either you're engaged or you're not.''

Rachel tipped up her chin. "We *aren't* engaged," she said in a firmer voice. "Not anymore."

"But, Lovebug…" Russell began.

She turned to him. "And how dare you waltz into my apartment one year after you waltzed out, without a word or a letter or even a telephone call!"

"I can explain."

Drew sat back, ready to enjoy the show. He knew from personal experience that nobody could do battle like Rachel Grant.

"Explain?" she repeated, her brown eyes snapping. "How do you explain practically abandoning me at the altar? We were supposed to get married last February. Until you pulled your disappearing act."

Married? Last February? No wonder she hated Valentine's Day. Which reminded him of his purpose here tonight. He was supposed to be persuading Rachel to drop the boycott. Instead he was acting like a bulldog protecting its turf. A gentleman would leave these two alone to work out their problems. Then again, a gentleman wouldn't have kissed Rachel to the point of passing out. So maybe he should stay. Just to size up the competition. Rachel, not Russell, he reminded himself firmly. His first priority needed to be the city of Love.

"Just hear me out, Lovebug," Russell said.

Drew's hand curled into a fist. If he called her that stupid pet name one more time…

"All right," she said, settling into the chair, a becoming flush on her cheeks. "Let's hear it."

Russell drained his wineglass, then poured himself

another. He cleared his throat twice, then sighed as he stared up at the ceiling. Drew half expected him to pull a violin out of his knapsack to accompany his sob story.

"Let me take you back to last February," Russell began, "so you can be inside my head."

That was the last place Drew wanted to be, but Rachel actually looked intrigued. He supposed that was the therapist in her. Which made him wonder if this Russell knew just what buttons to push.

"I didn't have any doubts about our marrying until I was awarded that grant from the entomology department. Suddenly I had enough money for my dream trip to Africa to study the dung beetle." Russell took a deep sip of wine. "Only how could I ask you to give up your career and come with me? You had your own career and patients that depended on you. And I couldn't imagine spending our honeymoon apart. Especially since I'd be gone for months."

"So you chose the dung beetle over me," Rachel said softly.

"I needed to find myself," Russell explained. "I didn't know what I wanted anymore. I wasn't sure I was ready for marriage. And I loved you too much to pretend."

Drew rolled his eyes, but Rachel seemed spellbound. She pulled her long legs up against her chest, wrapping her arms around them and resting her chin on her knees.

Russell sighed. "But instead of finding myself, I got lost."

"You mean emotionally lost?" Rachel asked.

Russell shook his head. "No, I mean actually lost. One of the guides took me into the bush on a beetle safari. But it started to rain, a monsoon, actually, and the Jeep got stuck in the mud. While the guide went to get help, I went to find shelter. My colleagues finally found me six months later living with a village of natives."

"That's incredible," Rachel said, exhaling.

Drew found it preposterous. This so-called story sounded more like a pile of…dung. But Rachel actually looked as if she believed him. Or wanted to believe him.

Russell nodded. "I know. But you can check it out with Professor Simmons from the university. They were all ready to give me up for dead when they came upon me in that village three weeks ago."

"Lucky for us," Drew said dryly.

"Getting lost in the bush was the best thing that ever happened to me," Russell said, gazing into Rachel's eyes. "Not only did I discover a rare new species of African dung beetle, but I discovered I loved you, Rachel. Truly and deeply. And now the most important thing to me is spending the rest of my life making you happy."

She twisted her hands in her lap. "This is all so…unexpected. I don't know what to say."

"Don't say anything. Yet." Russell got to his feet, picking up his knapsack. Then he looked at Drew, hitching his eyebrows toward the door. Sending him a silent message to get lost himself.

Drew just smiled as he settled deeper into the sofa. He wasn't planning on going anywhere.

Russell gave up and turned back to Rachel. He

pulled a small velvet box out of his knapsack. "This is for you," he said, handing it to her.

She held it in her hands, looking uncertain. "Gee, Russell, you shouldn't have."

"Open it," he prodded.

Drew set his jaw, wondering if Russell dressed like a drifter because he'd spent all his cash on a three-carat diamond ring. Or some exquisite emerald from an African mine. He carefully watched Rachel's expression as she opened the lid. If she smiled and squealed at the sight of some gaudy ring, then Drew was out the door.

But instead of joy, her face reflected puzzlement.

Rachel looked up at Russell. "It's a bug."

He bent down in front of her. "I know. The rare dung beetle I discovered near that village. Unknown until now, it's destined to make me famous among entomologists all over the world."

She stared down at the dead black bug in the red velvet box. "That's...wonderful, Russell."

"But you haven't even heard the best part," he exclaimed.

"You're going back to Africa?" Drew ventured.

Russell scowled at him, then turned back to Rachel. "No. The best part is that I named it for you. You're looking at the *Rachelona cyanella*."

Her eyes widened as she stared at the beetle. "Gee...I don't know what to say."

Russell moved closer to her, grasping her free hand in both of his. "Say you'll take me back, Rachel. Please let me prove to you how much I really love you."

When his chest began aching, Drew realized he

was holding his breath waiting for her answer. On the one hand, he thought Rachel much too sensible to fall for this guy's lame excuses. On the other hand, he knew plenty of women who fell for goofy intellectuals like the bug doctor.

Russell took the velvet box from her, carefully closing it, then setting it on an end table. "Don't say anything yet. I know this is all a shock to you. I probably should have called you as soon as I got back to civilization. But I wrote you a letter every day I spent in that village." He pulled a stack of ivory envelopes tied with a pink silk ribbon from his knapsack.

"They have hotel stationery in the bush?" Drew asked, not bothering to hide his skepticism.

"I wrote it on tree bark, then transcribed it onto paper later." He pushed the envelopes into her lap. "You can read these, then give me your answer. We'll have plenty of time to get reacquainted now that I'm back."

"Where are you staying?" Rachel asked.

Russell put on a little boy lost expression he'd obviously perfected wandering around in Africa. "I spent my last dime on a first-class ticket back to the States. I couldn't wait to be with you again. But since I won't start teaching back at the university until the summer session, I was hoping you'd let me camp out here."

"Here?" Rachel and Drew said at the same time.

"I travel light," he said, motioning to his knapsack. "I've learned to relinquish material things for what's really important, like love and friendship. I just want to fill my life and my heart with you."

Drew thought he might be sick. What did this guy do, memorize Hallmark cards in his spare time?

Rachel nibbled her lower lip. "But this apartment only has one bedroom."

Russell grinned. "Sounds perfect to me."

It sounded a little too cozy to Drew. It also made him want to wipe that smile off Russell's face. Preferably with his fist. But what right did he have to interfere with their relationship? Despite that soul-searing kiss, he didn't have any claim on Rachel.

Although he still needed to convince her to drop the boycott. That was the prime objective of this date. A date that wasn't going exactly as he planned.

He looked from Rachel to her love-struck fiancé as a new strategy formed in his mind. He didn't like it. In fact, he almost considered declaring her the winner in their endless Valentine's Day debate just so he could avoid going to this extreme. But that meant throwing in the towel, and Drew never quit competing until the last play of the game. Now he just needed to alter his game plan. He needed more time. More access to Rachel. He needed a reason to keep her in his life.

He needed…a roommate.

6

*Send me no flowers,
it just isn't done.
It's perfectly clear
I've already won.*

TWO DAYS LATER Rachel lay on the tweed sofa in her office while her best friend played therapist. "So do you think I'm paranoid?" she asked, staring up at the ceiling. She saw a dead bug in the fluorescent light fixture and vaguely wondered if she should give it to Russell for his birthday.

Or maybe a bug zapper. A gift that kept on giving.

Gina sat in the armchair, thumbing through a mercenary magazine in her search for the perfect hit man. "Paranoid? Just because your date asked your fiancé to move in? Of course not."

"My ex-fiancé," Rachel amended. "Although, I never gave him the ring back."

"How could you? He left the continent."

"Exactly. So we never officially broke it off." She rested her arms behind her head. "Isn't there some sort of statute of limitations on disappearing fiancés?"

Gina shrugged. "According to my research, a missing person can be legally declared dead after seven years. But I don't know about missing fiancés. Do you want me to look into it?''

''No,'' Rachel replied. ''I want you to help me figure out the motive behind Drew's suspiciously generous offer. Why would he offer a room in his house to a complete stranger?''

''Loneliness?''

Rachel grimaced at Gina. ''Please. The man needs a revolving door on his house to keep his girlfriends from bumping into each other. No, I think he's up to something.''

''But what? You told me he didn't even like Russell.''

''Well, he certainly didn't act like it. Making snide remarks when Russell was telling his story. He even stepped on Russell's knapsack.''

''Sounds like jealousy to me.''

Rachel rolled her eyes. ''That's ridiculous. We can't agree on anything. And he thinks I'm a kook.''

''But what about that kiss?''

Rachel gazed at her friend in astonishment. ''How did you find out? I never told you Drew kissed me last night.''

''Ve fake therapists have vays of making you talk,'' Gina slurred, in an atrocious German accent. ''Besides, you did tell me. Just now. I was referring to that kiss in the television parking lot.''

''Oh,'' Rachel replied, her cheeks growing warm.

Gina tapped her finger against the magazine. ''Out with it, Rach. What happened between you and the mayor last night? I want details. Lots of details. Since my love life's in the toilet, I have to live vicariously through you.''

"There's not much to tell," Rachel began, wondering how to describe a nuclear meltdown in her living room. "We kissed, Russell rang the doorbell and the date went downhill from there. Then they left together, leaving me alone in the apartment."

Gina arched a dark brow. "So which one did you want to stay?"

Rachel bit her lip, wishing she knew the answer. "Neither one, I suppose. Although I still have a lot of questions for Russell."

"You have to admit his *lost in the bush* story sounds a tad farfetched. How many entomologists do you know who disappear in search of the elusive dung beetle? For six months, no less."

Rachel stifled a giggle that she feared was closer to hysteria than humor. "I know. But Professor Simmons called me this morning and backed up everything Russell told me. He really was missing from the camp for six months. They finally found him in that village three weeks ago. Professor Simmons even saw the piles of tree bark love letters he'd written me."

"Wow. That's incredible. So is Russell still a hunk?"

Rachel nodded. "Yes. In a disheveled, scholarly, rough-around-the-edges kind of way."

Gina sighed as she fell back against the chair. "Just like Harrison Ford in those Indiana Jones movies."

Rachel nodded. "Exactly. Too handsome for his own good. Or mine."

"So maybe Drew is jealous. Maybe he couldn't stand the thought of you two alone together."

Rachel considered Gina's theory, then voiced a theory of her own. "Or maybe he wants to use Russell to get to me somehow."

Gina shook her head. "Men as handsome as Drew Lavery are usually not that smart. And they're definitely not as devious as women. Maybe there's no ulterior motive. Maybe he's just a nice guy doing you a favor."

"By keeping my fiancé for me until I decide if I want him back?" Rachel said skeptically.

"Ex-fiancé," Gina reminded her.

"And you're wrong about Drew," Rachel continued as if Gina hadn't spoken. "He's one of those rare exceptions of men with both brain and brawn. I wouldn't put anything past him."

"So what about Russell? Do you want him back?"

Rachel sighed. "Besides his looks, Russell's dedication to his career always appealed to me. I thought we'd be perfect together. But now I realize respect and admiration aren't enough. Ever since I met…"

"Drew?"

Rachel shook her head. "I don't know what I want. Believe it or not, I'm a little confused right now."

"I believe it," Gina said. "I saw all the Twinkie wrappers in your office wastebasket. Eat enough of those, my little cupcake, and soon neither one of them will want you."

Rachel scowled at her. "This is not helping. I need answers. Although…I think I just figured out why Drew offered Russell a place to stay."

Gina sat up in the chair. "Well, don't keep me in suspense."

"It's the boycott," Rachel said simply, wondering why she hadn't figured it out sooner. "He wants to use Russell as leverage. Maybe he thinks I'll be so grateful to him for offering my ex-fiancé a place to stay that I'll change my mind about boycotting Valentine's Day.''

Gina shook her head. ''That sounds pretty lame to me. I'm still voting for the jealousy theory. Drew couldn't stand the thought of you two alone together, so he sacrificed his home to the cockroach king.''

''Russell is into beetles now. He even named one for me. The *Rachelona cyanella*.''

''I always thought Russell was a little strange. I think you should go after the mayor.''

Rachel frowned. ''The mayor is in retreat, planning his next attack. I haven't heard a word from him since our date.''

Gina didn't say anything. Rachel glanced over to see her staring intently at the magazine. ''What is it?''

''A grenade that looks just like a pineapple,'' Gina said. ''Kurt loves pineapple. What if I sent him a fruit basket…''

''Forget it, Gina,'' Rachel said, just as the intercom buzzed on Rachel's desk.

She rose from the sofa, all those Twinkies rumbling in her stomach. Maybe she'd overdone it this time. She shouldn't have eaten that last box.

She punched the button on the intercom. ''Yes, Jodie?''

''Dr. Grant, there is a woman here to see you. A Mrs. Lavery.''

''I don't believe it,'' Gina exclaimed, throwing the magazine down. ''He's married! What a jerk! I knew he was too good to be true.''

The Twinkies settled like a stone in the pit of her

stomach. Mrs. Lavery? There had to be some mistake...

"*She's the mayor's mother,*" Jodie whispered over the intercom. "*Shall I tell her you're with a patient?*"

Rachel turned to Gina. "Can you believe it? *His mother.* He actually sent his mother to do his dirty work."

"You don't know that for sure."

"Can you think of another reason? I bet he sent her here as a spy, hoping to pump me for information. She's probably wired."

"Okay—now I think you are paranoid. You really think Drew would use his mother like that?"

Rachel closed her eyes, her head muddled from the events of the last few days. Her attraction to Drew completely baffled her. They had nothing in common. He was an uptight bureaucrat who only cared about the bottom line and she was a woman who dealt in emotions and followed her heart. So why couldn't she stop thinking about him?

Then there was Russell. She still couldn't believe he'd dropped into her life again. She hadn't stopped eating Twinkies since his return. *What did that mean?*

"I don't know what to think anymore," Rachel muttered.

"At least you can find out why Drew's mother is here to see you."

Static crackled over the intercom. "*Dr. Grant?*"

Rachel checked her watch. Forty-five minutes until her Transitions support group meeting. Plenty of time to interrogate the enemy. Or rather, the enemy's mother. She pressed the intercom button. "Please send Mrs. Lavery right in."

Gina settled deeper into the chair. "I think I should stay, just in case it gets ugly. After all, she might be here to get back at you for beating up her son."

"I didn't beat him up. We had a snowball fight. And I won."

"He ended up in the hospital!"

Rachel frowned at her. "He wasn't unconscious *that* long. The paramedics probably overreacted. Besides, he's fine now." At least, she hoped he was fine. The concussion had given him a case of selective amnesia. Maybe another complication had set in. Maybe Mrs. Lavery wanted revenge.

Rachel held her breath as the door opened, half expecting an older, mirror image of Drew Lavery, but with breasts. Instead a petite woman with chestnut brown hair, kind blue eyes and faint lines etched in her face stepped into the office.

"Dr. Grant?" Kate Lavery asked, looking at Gina seated in the therapist's chair.

Rachel hesitated just a moment, waiting to see if Drew's mother went for Gina's throat. Then she stepped forward. "I'm Rachel Grant."

Kate grasped her hand, giving it a gentle squeeze. "How very nice to meet you, Dr. Grant. I've heard so much about you."

"Please call me Rachel," she told her, assuming it was the least she could do after sending her son to the hospital. She didn't want to imagine what Drew had said about her. And then there were the newspaper articles and the television show.

"Rachel," Kate echoed, letting the name roll off her tongue. "How lovely. I think one of the Detroit

Lions fullbacks is married to a Rachel. I'll have to check my book."

Gina blinked up at her. "You have a book on the Detroit Lions football team?"

Kate sat down on the sofa. "I have several. They're my favorite NFL team. I've even sold houses to a couple of the linebackers. Big, hulking men." She smiled up at Rachel. "And so strong I think they could snap a leg in two like a toothpick."

Rachel swallowed. Was that a veiled threat? Beat up my son again and I'll send a linebacker after you?

Gina sat up straighter in her chair. "So do you follow all their games?"

Kate laughed. "Follow them? I've got season tickets. That's the first thing I told my lawyer I wanted in the divorce. They're great tickets, too. Right on the fifty-yard line."

"You're divorced?" Rachel asked, sitting down on the other end of the sofa. She suddenly realized how very little she knew about Drew. Only that he was the mayor, dead set against the boycott and a great kisser.

Kate nodded. "It got a little messy. My ex-husband sued me for joint custody."

"Of Drew?" Rachel asked, wondering how old he'd been at the time. Or did he have younger brothers and sisters?

Kate laughed. "No, of the football tickets. He wanted each of us to take one, but he never really liked football. In the end, I prevailed."

Gina dug into her purse. "Wow, I have to get the name of your lawyer."

Rachel just wanted to know the reason behind Kate

Lavery's unexpected arrival in her office. She couldn't help but like Drew's cheerful, vivacious mother. But that didn't mean she trusted her.

"My son is an excellent attorney," Kate said, "but I don't think he handles many divorce cases. Besides, he'd ask you where you got your referral. Then he'd find out I came here."

"Why are you here, Mrs. Lavery?" Rachel asked, her curiosity finally overcoming her.

Kate smiled. "I want to join the boycott."

CHARLIE STRODE into Drew's living room, a brown leather briefcase swinging from one hand. "I brought those contracts you wanted to look over." Then he tipped his nose in the air. "Is that your mother's famous lasagna I smell?"

"No," Drew replied, flipping on the overhead light. "It's frozen pizza."

"Isn't Monday lasagna night? Your mom makes the best lasagna in the world. I didn't agree to work overtime for frozen pizza," Charlie said, sounding puzzled as he snapped open his briefcase.

Drew loosened the tie around his collar, his mouth watering at the thought of his mother's lasagna. Maybe she was right. Maybe he'd gotten too used to having her around. He'd have to get out the directions to the dishwasher and figure out how to use it again.

"Does this mean your mom won't be cooking dinner for us...I mean, for you tonight?"

Drew shook his head. "Not tonight or any other night. She's joined some new group and told me she wouldn't be able to spend as much time here."

"She hasn't joined some cult, has she?"

Drew laughed. "Of course not. She's just not going to devote herself to me anymore. She's finally decided to move on with her life, and frankly, I couldn't be happier."

Charlie flinched. "You mean...no more Swedish meatballs? No more cranberry salad? No more caramel nut cake?"

"She copied out all the recipes if you want to borrow them."

Charlie shook his head in disbelief. "How can you be so cavalier about this? Your mother is abandoning us."

"You don't even live here. And Mom only came over here on Mondays, Wednesdays and Fridays."

Charlie sighed. "The most nutritious nights of my week."

A blood-curdling yell erupted somewhere above them. Charlie's eyes widened as he looked up the staircase. "What the hell was that?"

"Russell," Drew said, shuffling the contracts in his hands.

Charlie stared at him. "Who the hell is Russell?"

Before he could explain, Russell bounded down the stairs two steps at a time. He looked bedraggled and wild-eyed, his flannel shirt hanging out of his jeans. He skidded to a stop at the bottom of the stairs, hanging on to the banister for support.

"My *Megaloblatta longipennis*," he exclaimed, his eyes wide with apprehension. "It's gone."

Drew looked up from the contracts. "Your what?"

"It's the largest cockroach in the world," Russell explained, pacing back and forth. "It's from Japan and very rare. We have to call the police."

Charlie immediately jumped up on the sofa. "A giant cockroach? Forget the police. Call an exterminator!"

Drew stifled a smile at Charlie's reaction. His friend had an irrational fear of bugs. He'd quit the Boy Scouts just so he wouldn't have to face insects in the wild. "Don't worry, Dennison, they're all dead."

Charlie gulped. "You mean there's more than one?"

Russell sank down onto the bottom step. "I have the most extensive cockroach collection in the country. The *Megaloblatta longipennis* was the crowning jewel, coveted by all my colleagues." He stood up and headed toward the telephone. "One of them probably stole it. Just another case of entomologist envy. I'm calling the cops."

"Wait a minute, Russ," Drew said, another news headline flashing before his eyes: Mayor's House Full of Cockroaches. "Are you sure you didn't lose it somewhere?"

Russell rifled his hand through his blond hair. "Of course not. I always keep it in the special locked case with the rest of the collection. I left it open last night and now the Megaloblatta is gone."

Missy the cat suddenly scampered around the corner, tossing a suspicious, brown object in the air with her paw.

Russell looked on in horror. "My Megaloblatta!" He caught it in midair, then checked it for damage. Then he breathed a long sigh of relief. "Miraculously it seems to be in good condition."

Drew wished he could say the same about Charlie,

who looked more than a little green around the gills. He turned to Russell. "Maybe you'd better take it back upstairs and put it away. You can lock the case in your bedroom closet for safekeeping. Just don't lose the key."

"I'll guard it with my life," Russell said, cradling the dead bug in his hands as he ascended the staircase.

Charlie sank down onto the sofa. "Who is that guy? Don't tell me he's a friend of yours."

"Not exactly. He's Russell Baker, a soon-to-be famous entomologist and Rachel's fiancé."

"Rachel? Your Rachel?"

"She's not my Rachel," Drew said, even though that's exactly how he'd been thinking of her. Especially after Russell had arrived and tried to stake his claim.

"Of course she isn't," Charlie affirmed. "But I can't believe that guy is her fiancé."

"I think ex-fiancé is more accurate." Drew had spent enough time with Russell Baker to know for certain this man was all wrong for Rachel. "He abandoned her a year ago, on Valentine's Day."

Charlie nodded. "So that explains it."

"Now he's back with some cockamamy story, claiming he's madly in love with her. He even planned on moving in with her." Drew shook his head. "Can you believe the nerve of that guy? But before she could turn him down, I offered him a place here. I thought it might be a good way to keep tabs on the competition."

"By competition, do you mean Russell or Rachel?"

"Rachel, of course," Drew replied. "Stopping this boycott is my top priority."

Charlie eyed him shrewdly. "I hope you remember that, Drew. Especially since you plan to campaign for state attorney general in the next election." He shook his head. "Rachel and her radical ideas would make her poison as a politician's wife."

"Wife?" Drew sputtered, trying to ignore the images it brought to mind. Rachel Grant sharing his name, his house, his bed. He ran a finger around his shirt collar. "Who said anything about a wife? I'm not looking for a wife, remember? I've already got my hands full." His memory, now crystal clear, envisioned his hands full of Rachel last night. How warm and soft and tempting she'd been when he'd kissed her. How he'd never wanted to let her go.

"That's good," Charlie said. "Especially since you don't seem to have much influence with her." He straightened his tie. "Maybe I should give it a try. I've been known to distract a few women in my time."

"Forget it, Dennison," Drew snapped. "Rachel Grant is off-limits. We have a bet, remember? Fifty bucks says I convince her to drop the boycott by Valentine's Day. I still have one week left."

Charlie hitched a thumb toward the ceiling. "The question is, can you stand to live with Russell and his cockroach collection for that long?"

"I'll do whatever it takes," Drew said grimly.

"Wait just a minute." A smile slowly dawned on Charlie's face. "This is wonderful. You've just found yourself the perfect weapon, Lavery."

"Weapon?"

"The bug man. If Rachel falls in love with him again, what happens?"

"She's kookier than I thought?"

"No," Charlie exclaimed in a low voice. "If she falls head-over-heels for Russell, she'll be too wrapped up in romance to bother with the boycott. In fact, she'll probably be the first in line to *celebrate* Valentine's Day."

As much as he hated to admit it, Charlie's idea made sense. "I don't know. He doesn't seem like her type."

Charlie shrugged. "Hey, she fell for him once before. She was even engaged to the guy. There must be some sparks left. Now you just have to find a way to ignite them."

Drew's jaw dropped. "Me? I'm no matchmaker."

"But you know women. Just give good old Russ some pointers. You know, teach him a few of your old tricks. C'mon, Lavery it's for a good cause."

"I'll have to think about it," Drew said, resisting the idea of fixing Rachel up with another man. Especially since even the thought of her kissing another man made his gut clench. But Russell certainly had more to offer her than Drew. Love. Marriage. A world-famous cockroach collection.

Charlie shrugged. "You can always just pay me the fifty bucks from our bet now. Because unless you've got a better idea, this boycott is going to derail Valentine's Day in Love."

One week. One week to play Cupid for Rachel and Russell. The thought made him cringe. But what choice did he have if he wanted to stop the boycott?

The oven timer dinged, providing a welcome distraction. "Supper's on. I've got enough if you want to stay."

Charlie sighed. "Frozen pizza. I guess I can choke it down if you've got plenty of beer to go with it. Do you mind if I turn on the game? The Detroit Pistons are playing the Bulls tonight."

"Sure, go ahead," Drew said, heading for the kitchen. "And tell Russell it's time to eat."

By the time he came back from the kitchen with pizza and beer and paper plates, Russell was seated in his favorite recliner. Charlie still sat on the sofa, the remote control in his hand, an expression of horror frozen on his face.

"The Bulls must be winning," Drew concluded, setting down the beer.

"It's worse than that," Charlie said. "Look."

Drew turned his gaze to the television set. He recognized the face of television reporter Candi Conrad beaming at the camera, a raucous crowd gathering behind her. *"This is a special newsbreak brought to you by WKLV in Love, Michigan. A protest rally has begun here at the Cupid Fountain in downtown Love…"*

"Hey, there's Rachel," Russell exclaimed, pointing toward the television set. "Wow, she looks great! And get a load of that crazy woman climbing on top of the Cupid statue."

"What the hell is going on?" Drew muttered as he took a better look. Then he dropped the pizza. "That's my mom!"

7

Send me no flowers,
buy me no ring.
I'll be perfectly happy
just having a fling.

BY THE TIME HE ARRIVED downtown, Drew knew what he had to do. He fought his way through the crowd until he reached the epicenter of the rally. That's where he found Rachel.

She stood on a platform in front of the fountain, her cheeks a rosy red from the cold and her big brown eyes sparkling with excitement. Her silky blond hair was pulled back by oversize furry black earmuffs. Her long, black leather coat was cinched at the waist and her black boots came up to her knees. She clutched a bullhorn with a bulky red mitten, reciting her top ten reasons to boycott Valentine's Day.

"Reason number seven," she shouted to the enthusiastic crowd gathered around her, "those sappy love songs on the radio."

The crowd whooped and hollered, some waving signs with the anti-Valentine's logo emblazoned on them. A newspaper photographer jostled his way through the crowd, gleefully snapping pictures.

"Number eight," she called out, "red hearts on underwear—need I say more?"

"Call the fashion police!" shrieked one of the protesters.

Drew didn't see his mother anywhere. At least she wasn't still straddling the statue. He couldn't take another minute of this nonsense. "I need to talk to you," he yelled over the noise of the crowd, waving his arms to get Rachel's attention.

She smiled and waved back at him.

Drew cupped his hands around his mouth. "I said I need to talk to you!"

She shrugged and pointed to her earmuffs, indicating she couldn't hear him. "Number nine…equal opportunity for singles." The crowd hooted and clapped its hands in support, their applause muted by the thick mittens on their hands.

"Rachel, I need to talk to you right now!"

"What?" she mouthed, or at least, that's what he interpreted. The crowd shifted, enabling him to edge a little closer. "I want to talk to you."

Either she didn't hear him or she was ignoring him, and he had a sneaking suspicion it was the latter.

"And reason number ten…all that candy causes cavities."

The crowd exploded with laughter and muffled applause. Somebody started singing a chorus of "We Shall Overcome." Drew reached her at last, grasping her by the shoulders. "You're driving me crazy," he shouted.

"What?" she asked, leaning closer to him.

"I'm crazy about you." He'd just wanted to get her attention. Or at least, that's what he told himself.

He'd never said those words before. To any woman. He just wanted to test them out. Test himself. But instead of panicking at the words, he felt warm all the way down to his toes. Then he looked down at his shoes. Someone in the crowd had dumped their hot cocoa on the ground, soaking his white Nikes.

"I still can't hear you," she said, flipping off her earmuffs.

He took the bullhorn away from her before she could incite a riot. "I said, are you crazy?"

This time Rachel heard him. So did the rest of the crowd, judging by the gasps and the sudden hush falling over them. Too late, he realized his mistake. The bullhorn was still on and had picked up his words.

He turned to the crowd, among them several irate members of the chamber of commerce. "I've got this boycott situation completely under control," he said through the bullhorn. "Now why don't you just disperse calmly and quietly while I deal with Dr. Grant."

"Why don't you pick on somebody your own size?" shouted a malcontent in the crowd.

So much for diplomacy. "I'm not picking on anybody. Dr. Grant started this mess..." The sound of police sirens saved him from saying something stupid. While the protesters milled around in confusion, Drew took advantage of the opportunity to make his escape.

He grasped Rachel gently by the elbow, disengaging her from the crowd. She didn't look too happy about it, mouthing words that he probably didn't want to hear. Once they were at a distance from all the pandemonium, he heard her only too loud and clear.

"Listen, you big jerk, you can't drag me around

like some Neanderthal. Didn't your mother teach you any manners?''

He dropped her arm and whirled around to face her. ''Yes, let's talk about my mother. I saw her on television, climbing around on that Cupid statue. Did you brainwash her into joining this stupid boycott?''

''In the first place, this boycott isn't stupid. And in the second place, your mother came to me about joining the boycott. But why am I telling you this, you obviously sent her in as a spy.''

His jaw dropped, his amazement at her accusation quickly followed by chagrin that he hadn't thought of it himself. Then it all became clear. His mother just wanted to win the bet. She was siding with the enemy for a lousy fifty bucks! ''Where is she?'' he asked, looking around the crowd.

Shivering in the bitter cold, Rachel wrapped her arms around her body. ''She and Frank Anders went to the coffee shop on the corner to warm up. Crawling around on that stone statue is bone-chilling work.''

He shook his head. ''What was she even doing up there?''

Rachel pointed to the statue. ''Putting underwear on Cupid. Irma knitted him a pair of red drawers because she thinks it's indecent to have a naked statue in the town square. Especially in the middle of winter.''

Drew stared in disbelief at the statue, noticing for the first time the bright red boxer shorts hanging off of Cupid's stone waist. This was a living nightmare.

''So now you're protesting naked statues. What's next? A field trip to the art museum to paint clothes on all the nudes? Don't you have anything better to do with your time, Dr. Grant? Aren't there enough lunatics running around to keep you busy?''

She tipped her chin. "We don't call patients lunatics anymore. And I happen to think this Valentine's Day protest is important. See how many people showed up." She nodded toward the crowd.

Too many, by Drew's calculation. He needed to act fast. And the only plan he could come up with was the one Charlie had suggested earlier in the evening. Make Rachel forget about the boycott by rekindling her romance with her ex-fiancé.

His every instinct screamed against it, but he didn't have time to come up with an acceptable alternative. Besides, the sooner he got Rachel out of his system, the better. Even now he couldn't resist moving a step closer to her and rubbing his hands up and down her arms to warm her. "You're cold."

"I'm fr...fr...freezing," she said, her teeth chattering.

He opened his bulky overcoat and wrapped it around her so she was pressed up tight against his chest.

"What are you doing?" she asked, clearly torn between outrage at his presumption and the lure of his body heat.

"I'm keeping you warm so the crowd doesn't turn on me. They already don't like me. Can we just talk like this for a few minutes?"

"I guess so," she said, burrowing into his warmth. "Just make it quick."

He inhaled the herbal scent of her hair, and felt the soft curves of her body pressed up against him. He was more than warm now. He kept his arms wrapped around her, enveloping them both in his thick wool overcoat. "That's better," he murmured against her earmuff. "Much better."

"I'm not so cold now," she said, nestling her cheek against his shoulder.

"Me, neither," he said huskily, enjoying Rachel in his arms. Enjoying it way too much. He didn't want Rachel Grant in his life. He couldn't afford Rachel in his life. And the city couldn't afford any more of these anti-Valentine's Day shenanigans. It was time to get his mind back on business.

"I was hoping," he said, before his resistance weakened even further, "that you might consider coming to my house for dinner sometime this week."

She pulled back slightly to look up at him. "Dinner at your house? That sounds a little fishy. What are you up to now, Drew?"

He pressed his lips together. They felt chapped from the cold air. For one brief moment, he thought about warming them on Rachel's mouth. But that wouldn't accomplish anything except filling his head with fantasies. Impossible dreams that could never come true.

"Look, Rachel, I know I've been kind of a jerk lately. I really want to make it up to you." That was true. He had been a jerk; ambushing her on television and forcing her into a date. But would reuniting her with Russell really make her happy? Drew didn't want to think about it.

"I don't know…" she said softly, nibbling on her lower lip.

"How about tomorrow night?" he said, hoping to catch her at a vulnerable moment. "Around seven?"

He held his breath, hoping she would let down her defenses and agree to dinner. Then Russell could make his move. He tried to ignore the image that evoked in his mind. But the more he thought about it, the more he hoped she refused his goodwill gesture. Maybe he'd made the wrong decision. Maybe he should give it some time, think it over before he did anything rash.

But Rachel didn't give him a chance. Before he could withdraw his invitation, she came to a decision.

"All right, Drew," she said huskily, stepping out of his arms. "I'll see you tomorrow night."

Then she turned and walked away, leaving Drew to wonder if it was possible to get frostbite from the inside out.

GINA SAT ON THE FLOOR in Rachel's bedroom, her back propped against the foot of the bed. "It's after midnight, Rach," she said, stifling a yawn. "Can I go home now?"

Rachel stood in front of her closet, rifling through her clothes. "I know it's late, but I really need your opinion."

"For a date with Drew? I still can't believe you agreed to it. Don't you despise the man?"

"Despise is a strong word." Rachel drew out a bright red-and-white polka dot dress, then turned around and held it up to her. "Well?"

Gina squinted. "Makes me dizzy."

Groaning, she hung it back in the closet. "Drew and I have had our share of disagreements, but I think he's really trying to make amends. The least I can do is meet him halfway." She held up the topaz blue wool dress she'd worn on her date with Gordon. "How about this?"

"Boring with a capital *B*," Gina said, stretching her arms above her head. "I can tell this is going to take a while. Do you have anything to munch on?"

"There's a box of Twinkies on the nightstand."

"Speaking of Twinkies, how's Russell?"

Rachel pulled out a black dress with a long slit up the back, eyeing it critically. It was one of her favorites, but probably too formal for this occasion. "Russell?"

Gina tore open the cellophane wrapper containing a pair of Twinkies. "You remember him. The tall blond hunk who made your name immortal among beetle lovers everywhere."

"Of course I remember him. What about him?" She pulled a peach silk pantsuit from the back of her closet. It had possibilities, but she didn't have any shoes to go with it. She frowned at the rainbow of shoes on the shoe rack on her closet floor. Why hadn't she ever bought peach-colored shoes in case of an emergency?

"What about him?" Gina echoed in disbelief. "Rach, the guy is still crazy about you. Did you read those love letters he wrote to you?"

"I skimmed them." She turned toward Gina, holding a pink wool suit in front of her.

Gina shook her head. "Too old-fashioned." She broke a Twinkie in half, licking the creamy white filling in the center of the cake. "Well, maybe you'd better take a closer look. I read a couple of those letters and had to take a cold shower. He *really* wants you back."

"I know," she said, rejecting one outfit after another, until she reached the end of the clothes rod. "He's called a couple of times."

"And?"

Beginning to panic, Rachel stared into her closet. "And I don't have anything decent to wear! What am I going to do? I've got a full schedule tomorrow so I don't have time to go shopping."

Gina finished off the last of her Twinkie.

"What's going on? The last outfit you wore on a date with Drew would have been rejected by the Salvation Army. Why all the fuss and worry about this date?"

Abandoning her closet for the moment, Rachel plopped down on the stool next to her dresser. "I'm not worried. I just want to look nice. Maybe I can go shopping during my lunch hour tomorrow."

"Skip lunch? Now I know it's serious." Gina smiled as she licked cake crumbs off her fingers. "When did it happen?"

"When did what happen?" Rachel asked, studying her fingernails. Maybe she'd make time for a manicure, too.

"When did you stop thinking of Drew Lavery as the enemy?"

Rachel looked at her. "He's still the enemy. I just think this dinner is his attempt at a cease-fire. Maybe he's even ready to surrender."

"He's not the only one. Do you realize this is the first *second* date you've been on since Russell went AWOL last February?"

Rachel started to protest, then realized Gina was right. "But this really doesn't count as a date. The only reason Drew and I are seeing each other at all is because of the boycott.''

"Please. If it doesn't count, then why are you on the verge of a fashion anxiety attack? Why don't you just admit you're falling for the guy?''

"Because I don't want to fall for him," Rachel insisted, knowing it might already be too late. "I'm happy with my life just the way it is. I don't have room for romance.''

"Spoken like a true coward.''

Rachel's jaw dropped. "What's the supposed to mean?''

"It means you've been pushing guys away ever since Russell dumped you. It's not healthy.''

"At least I'm not planning to send him a gift-wrapped boa constrictor for his birthday!" she exclaimed, referring to Gina's latest murder scheme.

"I'm not going through with the snake plan. It would put a squeeze on my budget.''

Rachel reached for a Twinkie. But Gina grabbed the box and held it out of reach. "No more Twinkies until you admit the truth. You're afraid to fall in love again.''

"This is silly. I am not afraid of anything. I just happen to believe you don't have to be in love to be happy.''

"I know. It's your mantra. And, I'm actually starting to believe it, too. But believing it doesn't mean you have to be single for the rest of your life. Maybe being with Drew can make you even happier.''

"I'd be ecstatic if you'd just please pass me the Twinkies.''

Gina held up a package in the air. "Not until you

admit you've been using Twinkies as a substitute for love. When Russell left, you ate them to fill the void. And now, since Drew entered the picture, you're fighting your attraction to him by turning to Twinkies instead.''

"I think you've been reading too many pop psychology books."

"I think I'm right. You're afraid to fall in love with Drew Lavery."

"That's ridiculous. I haven't known him long enough to fall in love." Rachel didn't want to talk about Drew anymore. She wanted Twinkies.

"There's no timetable for falling in love. Some people take months, some weeks, and some only seconds. Why don't you just admit you're falling for him?"

"Because I don't want to fall for him," Rachel exclaimed. "I'm not sure I can trust him. I've never known a man so focused on getting what he wants. And he really wants to stop this boycott."

"Maybe his focus has changed. What if he wants you?"

Rachel swallowed. Was that possible? Just the idea of Drew wanting her, with no agenda and no ulterior motives, suddenly made her feel all giddy. It was also scaring her to death. "So what should I do?"

Gina tossed her a package of Twinkies. "I say go for it. If it doesn't work out, we can split the cost of the boa constrictor and wreak our revenge."

Rachel gazed at the package of Twinkies in her hand, now realizing what she really wanted. She tossed the Twinkies back to Gina. "Deal."

EARLY THE NEXT MORNING, Drew told Russell he had a date with the girl of his dreams.

"You're making dinner for me and Rachel?" Russell sat at the kitchen table, his spoon poised in midair over his Fruit Loops.

"The works, Russ," Drew replied, spreading cream cheese over his toasted bagel. "It will be a dinner she never forgets."

"And she's coming tonight?"

"At seven o'clock sharp. Bet you can hardly wait."

Russell put his spoon down. "Well, actually, I'd planned to watch a special on PBS tonight. They're rebroadcasting 'The Bugs From Brazil.' It's a great show."

Drew stared at him in disbelief. "You mean, you'd choose a rerun over Rachel?"

Russell shrugged. "I just think tomorrow night would work better for me."

"Tomorrow night? You're lucky she even agreed to have dinner with you at all. If you cancel on her now, you can just kiss a reconciliation with her good-bye."

Russell hesitated, plainly torn by the choice before him. At last he said, "You're right. Besides, you've got a VCR, so I can tape the show."

Drew breathed a silent sigh of relief. He never thought he'd have to talk Russell into this date. "Whatever. Now forget about the television show. I need you to help out a little here."

Russell swallowed his cereal. "Gee, Drew, I'm not much of a cook, although I'm pretty good with a campfire. If you've got enough firewood and some hot dogs, I can try to start a blaze in the backyard.''

Drew put down his bagel. Russell was missing the importance of this dinner. ''This isn't a hot dog date. Rachel deserves only the best. This is the moment you've been waiting for, Russ. A romantic dinner for two so you can let her know exactly how you feel.''

Russell nodded. ''You're absolutely right. I've already wasted enough time. I need to sweep Rachel off her feet.''

''Exactly. Make this a night she'll never forget. Wear a suit and tie. Shave. Maybe even put on some shoes.''

Russell groaned. ''The only shoes I've got are my hiking boots. And the only clothes I've got with me are the jeans and T-shirts in my duffel bag.''

''Well, I can loan you some money…''

''Absolutely not,'' Russell interjected. ''I don't take charity. Besides, I already owe you for letting me stay here and fixing me up with Rachel. Winning her back is my top priority.''

''Face it, Russ. You can't win her back wearing a T-shirt that says, Bugs Rule!''

Russell frowned down at his wrinkled T-shirt. ''Maybe you're right. Do you have a suit I could borrow?''

''Sure,'' Drew said, telling himself it was for a good cause. Rachel deserved to be happy. She deserved to have a man who put her first in his life. Russell seemed committed to doing that now. At least, most of the time. Drew certainly couldn't do it. He had plans. Career goals he'd set for himself. Goals that had been important to him at one time. And they'd be important to him again, he assured himself, as soon as he got Rachel Grant out of his system.

"How about dress shoes?" Russell enquired. "I wear size ten."

"I wear size eleven."

Russell grinned. "Close enough. Hey, I really appreciate this."

"No problem."

Russell dug happily into his Fruit Loops. Then he looked up. "Oh, by the way, can I borrow a razor?"

"Upstairs bathroom medicine cabinet," Drew replied, determined to draw the line at his toothbrush. "And don't worry about a thing. I'll set the table in the dining room and cook a delicious dinner for two in the kitchen. You won't even know I'm here."

Russell set down his spoon. "You can cook? Then how come we've had frozen pizza for supper every night this week?"

"Because pizza is convenient and goes so well with beer." Drew picked up his bagel. "Mom left me all her best recipes, and she's a great cook. All I've got to do is follow directions. How hard can that be?"

8

Send me no flowers,
our romance is done.
Now you can enjoy
dinner for one.

LATER THAT EVENING, Drew slid a pan of garlic bread
under the broiler, then checked his mother's recipe
card. *Broil garlic bread for five minutes.* This was a
recipe he could handle. Just spread butter on the bread
and sprinkle with garlic powder, parmesan cheese and
oregano. His mouth began to water at the fragrant
aroma.

Now if only the rest of the recipes had been so
easy to follow. He lifted the lid of the clam sauce,
frowning down at the lumpy contents. Maybe it
needed more heat. He turned the burner up to high,
then checked the linguine. It was boiling nicely. He'd
just leave it there so it would stay nice and hot until
it was time to serve it.

He wanted everything to be perfect for Rachel.

He pulled the zucchini casserole out of the refrig-
erator, glad he'd talked his mother into making it for
him. He could hardly spell zucchini, much less figure
out how to cook it. But it looked delicious through

the plastic wrap covering the baking dish. He'd pop it into the oven as soon as the garlic bread was ready.

That left the cheese ball and dessert to prepare. He pulled the cream cheese out of the freezer, then hurried over to the stove to check on the seven-minute frosting. It had been cooking fifteen minutes and still didn't look done. He gave it a quick stir with a rubber spatula just as the doorbell rang. A ripple of panic washed over him. She was early.

"Russell," he shouted. "Get the door."

No sound from upstairs. Russell was obviously still up there trying to figure out how to tape "The Bugs From Brazil" on the VCR. A woman like Rachel at the door and all this guy wanted was to watch foreign bugs crawl across the screen.

The doorbell rang a second time, and Drew quickly wiped his hands on a dish towel before heading for the living room. He yelled for Russell once more, then pulled open the front door.

"Hello, Drew." Rachel smiled at him as she stepped into the foyer. She took off her leather coat, draping it over her arm.

Her short, sapphire blue dress clung to her body in all the right places, revealing just enough skin to tempt him into wanting to see more. Her blond hair was swept up loosely in the back, sexy tendrils escaping to frame her face. She wore strapless high heels that accentuated her long, slender legs. Legs that made his mouth go dry.

She was gorgeous. Too gorgeous for Russell. Drew barely resisted the urge to slam the door in her face and call off the dinner. Russell didn't deserve a woman like her, especially when Drew wanted her all for himself.

"I hope I'm not too early."

"You're right on time," he muttered, realizing he was too late. Too late to correct the biggest mistake he'd ever made in his life.

RACHEL STOOD IN THE FOYER, a sense of déjà vu washing over her. She'd been here four days ago, nervously hoping she had the wrong house so she wouldn't have to go through with their date. A date that had climaxed with that bone-melting kiss.

Now she was back, but under completely different circumstances. This time she really wanted to be here. She shifted in her high heels, unnerved by the way Drew was staring at her. She couldn't help staring, either. Her date for the evening was dressed in blue jeans and a long-sleeved chambray shirt, with a frilly white apron tied around his waist. He held a rubber spatula in one hand and clearly didn't realize he had frosting smeared on his face.

On impulse, she reached out and wiped the small smudge off his cheek with one finger, then brought it to her mouth. "Mmmm...delicious."

His gaze followed her finger. He swallowed hard as she sucked the frosting into her mouth. "You have to leave," he said roughly.

"What?"

"You have to leave...your coat here," he muttered, grabbing her coat and turning around to hang it on the hall tree.

Before she could question his odd behavior, she heard someone on the stairway.

"Hey, Drew," Russell called, rambling down the stairs, "I borrowed your gold cuff links, too. These sleeves are a little long."

Rachel blinked in surprise at her ex-fiancé. She'd never seen him look so…formal. He wore a gray pin-striped suit that looked identical to the one Drew had worn on the television show. The jacket hung loosely on Russell's shoulders, but went well with the red silk tie and the white oxford shirt. The pants dragged a little on the floor, but not enough to cover the sight of the shoes slipping on his heels.

Despite his baggy clothes, he looked remarkably handsome. He'd shaved, revealing that deep cleft in his chin she'd always loved. He'd also gotten his hair trimmed.

Russell, her one-time Prince Charming, looked like Cinderella on the way to the ball. And Drew, with his apron and rubber spatula wand, was apparently the fairy godmother.

"Hey, Rach," Russell said when he saw her. "You look good enough to eat."

Drew scowled at Russell as he wiped his hands on his apron. "Can you wait until dinner? It's almost ready."

"Sure thing," Russell said, sliding his arm around Rachel's waist. "Isn't he a great guy, getting the two of us together like this?"

"The two of us?" Rachel echoed, wondering if Russell had the wrong impression. "Drew invited me here for dinner."

"Right," Russell replied with a nod. "He told me about it this morning. He knows my budget is pretty tight, so I can't afford to take you out anywhere. He even offered to cook us dinner.''

Rachel closed her eyes, feeling like the biggest fool in Love. Drew didn't want her, he just wanted to play matchmaker. But that didn't make any sense. She opened her eyes and looked at Drew, feeling slightly dizzy. ''You're cooking dinner for…me and Russell?''

''Most of the great chefs of the world are men,'' he said, waving his spatula in the air, ''so I think I can handle one dinner. After all, I do have a college degree.''

She didn't need a college degree to smell something burning. Maybe the concussion had affected his sense of smell. A smoke alarm went off somewhere, the shrill warning signal echoing throughout the big house.

Drew's eyes widened in horror. ''My garlic bread!'' He raced for the kitchen, his apron strings flying.

Russell smiled down at her, grasping her hands in his. They felt warm and callused. The hands of a man who had handled hundreds of insects. ''I'm so glad you're here, Rach,'' he said, over the piercing wail of the smoke alarm. ''It'll be just like old times.''

Great. She'd wanted this dinner to spark a new start with Drew and instead she got stuck with leftovers. How could she tell Russell she hadn't come here to rekindle their romance? Especially when he looked so hopeful, so handsome and so happy to see her?

When he'd first shown up on her doorstep last Saturday night, she'd been too shocked to know her true feelings. Then she'd had that Twinkie relapse. She still liked Russell and admired his dedication to his profession. And she still felt that flicker of physical attraction. But after one date with Drew, and that sizzling kiss, she knew a mere flicker wasn't enough for her anymore. Russell Baker had been her first love, but that love simply hadn't lasted. At least not for her. Part of her was even grateful that he'd taken off last February, before they'd both made a dreadful mistake.

She looked up into his eyes, not wanting to hurt him despite the way he'd abandoned her. But the words stuck in her throat. Maybe she'd wait until after dinner. Men always seemed to take bad news better on a full stomach.

He led her into the dining room and pulled out her chair. The table looked nice, even with the paper plates.

"I'd like to propose a toast," Russell said, pouring them both a glass of red wine. "To the *Rachelona cyanella*, the most beautiful beetle on earth, named for the most beautiful woman on earth."

She took a sip of wine, dismally seeing her future stretched out before her. Instead of having children, she'd be godmother to a beetle. Somehow, that wasn't enough.

Drew walked into the dining room just as the smoke alarm shut off. He placed a platter on the table. "Here are the appetizers."

Russell frowned down at the platter. "I thought you were making a cheese ball?"

"Change of plans," Drew snapped. "The cream cheese sort of...exploded when I tried to thaw it in the microwave. I guess I should have taken off that foil wrapper. But I'm sure you'll enjoy these even more.'' Then he headed back into the kitchen.

Rachel looked down at the bite-size, piping hot hors d'oeuvres in front of her. ''What are they?''

Russell sighed. ''Looks like he went with the frozen pizza again. He must have used cookie cutters to cut them into these little shapes.'' He picked a star-shaped appetizer and popped it into his mouth. ''Yep, Papa Pepe's Pepperoni Pizza. I'd recognize that cardboard crust anywhere.''

Rachel chose a pizza triangle, nipping off a little corner. ''Why is Drew doing all this?''

Russell shrugged. ''I guess he's just a genuinely nice guy. He seems really anxious to see us get back together.''

Rachel tried to ignore the twinge of disappointment deep inside her. How could he want that after their date? After that kiss? She gnawed at her pizza, worrying that she'd scared him off. Maybe he knew she was attracted to him. Maybe he wanted to distract her with Russell. Only she didn't want Russell. She wanted…well it didn't matter what she wanted anymore. It had all been a silly fantasy anyway. She put down the uneaten portion of her pizza appetizer as Drew walked back into the dining room.

''I've got some good news and some bad news,'' he announced, looking a little haggard. ''The good news is I managed to save the garlic bread.''

''And the bad news?'' Russell asked.

''The plastic wrap melted all over the zucchini casserole and the clam sauce is stuck to the bottom of the saucepan. Since I'm going to need a chisel to get it out, I improvised again.'' He placed a bowl of lumpy red sauce on the table. "I'll be right back with the linguine."

Russell stared down at the bowl after Drew left. "What is it?"

Rachel looked from the sauce to the appetizers and back again. "It looks like he scraped the topping off of Papa Pepe's Pepperoni Pizza and added some water."

"I should have gone with the hot dogs," Russell said under his breath. Then he smiled at Rachel. "But just being here with you makes it all worth it. I've really missed you this last year, Lovebug."

Rachel took another sip of her wine, trying to wash down the aftertaste of the appetizers. Maybe she should tell him it was over now. If she was lucky, he'd kick her out of the house and she wouldn't have to eat any more of Drew's cooking. "Listen, Russell…"

Drew came into the dining room, carrying a bowl of linguine and a basketful of garlic bread. "Hope you're hungry. I scraped all the black stuff off the top of the bread, so it should taste fine." He picked up a few strands of linguini with the tongs. The entire mass came out of the bowl in one solid lump.

Rachel bit back a smile at the bewildered expression on his face.

"Guess it got a little sticky," he said, trying to separate the strands with a fork. Finally he took a knife, cutting the lump of linguini down the middle. He placed half of it on Rachel's plate and gave Russell the rest of it.

She stared down at the clump of noodles on her plate, wondering how she'd ever gotten into this mess. She'd spent two hundred dollars on a new dress just to choke down a plateful of overcooked linguine.

"Maybe if you put on some of the sauce, it will loosen up the noodles," Drew suggested.

She couldn't face another bite of Pape Pepe's Pepperoni Pizza. "Actually I like mine plain," she said, bravely sawing off a chunk. She chewed the dry, sticky noodles. And chewed. And chewed some more.

If Drew would stop staring at her, waiting for her reaction, she could discreetly spit it into her napkin. Instead she had to swallow and make a grab for her wineglass.

"Well?" he asked, his handsome face full of expectation.

The lump of linguine lodged in her throat. She swallowed hard, forcing it down. "I've never had anything like it."

He smiled. "Great. I've got more in the kitchen."

She shook her head, pushing her plate away. "I want to save room for dessert."

"My dessert!" he exclaimed, making a mad dash for the kitchen as the smoke alarm sounded again.

"Hey, this stuff isn't so bad with the pizza sauce," Russell said, sawing his way through the linguine. "Although the rest of this meal is a disaster."

The perfect opening. "Maybe it's a sign. I don't think we're meant to be together, Russell."

"But I love you."

She licked her dry lips. "The problem is I don't love you. Not anymore."

He forked up a clump of linguine. "You're just still angry about my trip to Africa. I realize you need some time, Lovebug. And I'm willing to give you all the time you want.''

He looked incredibly cheerful for a man facing rejection. Or rather, ignoring her rejection. She wanted to make it clear, so they could both move on with their lives. "Russell, I don't want to hurt you."

"Ouch!" He shot out of his chair.

Rachel's breath caught in her throat. "What is it? What's the matter?"

"I just cut myself on the knife. It's nothing."

Nothing but blood oozing out of his finger. If Drew came in here and saw it, he'd land face first in the linguine.

Rachel grabbed her napkin and hurried over to him. "Here, wrap this around it."

"I appreciate your concern, but it's really no big deal, Lovebug." He brushed off her first-aid attempts. "It's just a little cut. When I was in Africa, I accidentally got my leg sliced open with a machete. Now *that* was serious."

"This is serious, too," she exclaimed. "Drew is a little queasy about blood."

He placed his uninjured hand on his stomach. "I'm starting to feel a little queasy myself."

"You don't understand. The last time he saw blood, he actually passed out."

Russell rose to his feet, twisting the paper napkin around his index finger. "Gee, that's awful. I'll go upstairs and put a bandage on it right away. Maybe I should stay up there for a while...watch a little television." He glanced at Rachel. "You know, just until the bleeding stops."

"I think that's a good idea."

By the time Drew came back into the dining room, Rachel was alone, trying to hide all the linguine still left on her plate under her napkin.

Drew halted in the doorway. "Where's Russell?"

"Upstairs," Rachel replied, putting down her fork. She didn't know if she could stomach dessert. "He'll be right back."

"Oh...good." Drew cleared his throat. "Well, I cremated the cake, but I came up with an emergency standby."

She was almost afraid to look. If it was frozen pizza with whipped cream on top, she was definitely passing.

Instead he set down a plate filled with cinnamon toast hearts. "Toast is my specialty." He picked up a piece and bit into it.

She suddenly couldn't sit at Drew's table anymore, pretending she didn't have feelings for him. Not when he smiled at her that way, and looked so good, and had a trace of cinnamon-sugar topping on his lips that she desperately wanted to lick off.

"Try it," he said, taking another bite. "It's delicious."

She moistened her lips with her tongue, knowing the only thing she craved was him. She took a deep breath, drawing on all her willpower. "I can't."

He rolled his eyes. "Is it because I cut them into little hearts? I think that's taking this boycott a little too seriously. Here," he said, breaking a cinnamon toast heart in two. "Now try it."

He seemed to be an expert at breaking hearts. She ignored both the fractured heart on her plate and the one in her chest. "I think I'd better go check on Russell. He wasn't feeling well."

"Wait," he said, before she could make her escape. "About Russell..."

"What about him?"

He hesitated for a moment. "I think you two should take your time. Don't rush into anything. Not that Russ isn't a...nice guy."

"He's the smartest man I've ever met."

Drew scowled. "I don't know about that..."

"It's true." Rachel pushed her dessert plate away. "He's also kind and caring. A great conversationalist. And he always made me feel special."

Drew tossed his napkin onto the table. "I still think you should be careful. Russell is a little..."

"A little...what?"

"Shy."

Shy? Russell Baker? The same man who proposed marriage to her over the loudspeaker at the National Insect Symposium? The man who sang "My Girl" a cappella in front of one hundred people at their engagement party? The man who suggested honeymooning at a nudist beach so they could be at one with nature?

Rachel smiled tightly. "You don't know Russell very well yet. He's very outgoing."

Drew nodded and reached for another cinnamon toast heart. "Right. I just meant he probably feels a little rusty in the romance department. You don't want to put any pressure on him. I'd go slow if I were you. Very, very slow."

Two kisses and he thought she was a sex maniac?

"Don't get me wrong," Drew continued. "I think

he's a great guy. You two make a cute couple.'' He coughed then, choking on a piece of toast.

She shoved her glass of wine at him, and he took a deep swallow before recovering himself. "It comes down to this... You need some romance in your life, Rachel. Now Russell may not be the right man for you, but..."

"But it's really none of your business." More than ready to end this charade, she pushed her chair back from the table. Russell might be disappointed, but it sounded like it had all been Drew's idea anyhow. *Drew's idea?* She looked up at him as his strategy suddenly became clear. "Or is this about business, Mr. Mayor? Are you hoping I'll fall in love with Russell and forget about the boycott?"

"Let me explain..."

She shook her head in disbelief. "Do you really think I'm that gullible?" She didn't wait for his answer. Instead she grabbed her purse and stormed out of the dining room before she did something she might regret.

"Rachel, wait!" he called after her.

She turned on her heel. How stupid she'd been to think he cared about anything other than derailing this boycott. "Forget it, Drew. You'd better just get used to the taste of defeat. And if you want a sample, just eat some of that linguine!"

She stormed out the front door, too angry to even notice the cold. She heard the crunch of snow behind her, but didn't slow down. Drew finally caught up with her at the curb where she'd parked her car. "You forgot your coat."

She wrenched it out of his grasp. "And you forgot

I've got a good arm, so unless you want another snowball sandwich, you'd better get out of my way."

He moved in front of her, blocking the car door. "Look, tonight didn't turn out like I'd planned."

"Me, neither. Now move it."

"Not until you hear what I have to say."

"If this is about the boycott..."

"It's about us."

Avoiding his gaze, she shrugged into her coat. "There is no us!"

He moved a step closer to her. "Maybe I want there to be."

She narrowed her eyes. "Right. That's why you arranged this romantic dinner for me and Russell. And now that Plan A didn't work, you're ready to move to Plan B. Is seducing the opposition one of your usual tactics, Mayor, or do you only use it as a last resort?"

"Come inside and let me explain."

"I'd rather choke down another plate of that lousy linguine."

Drew raked his fingers through his hair. "Tonight was a mistake. A big mistake."

"You're absolutely right. I never should have agreed to come over here." She pushed past him to open her car door, anxious to get as far away from him as possible. "But don't worry, Drew, I never make the same mistake twice."

THE NEXT DAY, Drew sat in the corner deli with Charlie, staring dismally at the pastrami and rye in front of him. "I really blew it."

Charlie nodded happily. "Yep, I slaughtered you

at racquetball today. My game has really improved these last couple of weeks.''

"No, I mean I blew it with Rachel last night. I doubt she'll ever speak to me again."

"Hey, forget about her." Charlie grabbed a handful of potato chips off Drew's paper plate. "There's a great basketball game on tonight. And we've got the Miss Valentine pageant coming up in two days. Life is good."

"I can't forget about her," Drew replied, shoving his plate away. "That's the problem."

"You're taking this boycott too seriously. It's inflicted some damage on the town's economy, but I think we can recover. The parade entries are slowly trickling in. And all the hotels are booked for the Valentine's Day weekend, so it hasn't adversely affected the tourist trade."

Drew leaned forward in his chair. "You don't get it, Dennison. I'm not talking about the boycott. I'm talking about Rachel. I can't stop thinking about her. I can't stop dreaming about her. And I can't believe I tried to fix her up with the bug doctor."

Charlie lowered his sandwich. "What do you mean, tried? I thought you had it all worked out."

"Me, too. It seems I overestimated my cooking skills and underestimated my feelings for Rachel."

Charlie shook his head. "Feelings for Rachel? Wait just a minute. You can't fall for the leader of the boycott. It would be political suicide."

He sighed. "Don't worry. After last night, I don't think she ever wants to see me again."

Charlie looked relieved. "It's probably just a case of wanting what you know you can't have. The forbidden fruit syndrome. And let's face it, Rachel is a challenge to you. You've never had so much trouble with a woman before.''

"Trouble is right," Drew agreed. "I need to look at this logically. She's trying to bankrupt the town. She's given me a concussion. And she's trying to corrupt my mother.''

Charlie stopped eating. "Kate? What happened?"

Drew rubbed the back of his neck. "She didn't come home last night. I tried calling her earlier in the evening about her linguine recipe and left a message on her machine. She didn't get back to me until this morning. She's spending all her time with her new boycott buddy, Frank Anders.''

"Kate's got a boyfriend?"

He shrugged. "How should I know? She never comes over to the house anymore. And I'm really getting sick of frozen pizza. My life is a mess. I don't know what I want anymore." Only he did know. He wanted Rachel. He couldn't concentrate on work anymore. It just didn't energize him the way she did. He'd always thought of love and marriage and family as distractions. But maybe he had it backwards. Maybe committing your entire adulthood to a career was a distraction. Especially if it kept you from focusing on the truly important things in life.

"Just hang in there, buddy," Charlie said, picking up the pastrami and rye. "Two more days and I predict you'll forget all about Dr. Rachel Grant.''

"What happens in two days?"

"The Miss Valentine contest. A bevy of Love's most beautiful women competing for the title and the attention of the head judge. Sounds like the perfect cure for what ails you.''

Drew shook his head. ''I don't know, Dennison. After last night, I'm afraid it might be a permanent condition.''

Charlie bit into a pickle. ''Think positive and just concentrate on the pageant. We'll find you a beautiful girl who can cook and all your troubles will be over.''

*
*
*
*
*
*

ON FRIDAY EVENING, Rachel and her merry band of
protesters stood outside the backstage door at the
Miss Valentine beauty pageant. They were all dressed
in black, ready to embark on their mission.

"It's not too late to back out," Rachel said in a
low whisper. "This could get ugly."

"Let's hope so," Kate Lavery said, rubbing her
hands together. "I'm ready to rumble."

"No violence," Rachel reminded them. "We're
only here to make a statement. Now let's take our
positions." She checked her list. "Kate, you and Irma
are in charge of the picketers outside the front entrance of the building. Frank, you and Lacie take the
rest of the group and seat them in strategic places
throughout the auditorium. We want to be in view of
the judges and the television cameras."

"What about you, Dr. Grant?" Kate asked, her
dark hair tucked under a Detroit Red Wings ball cap.

"Gina and I are going backstage to the contestants
waiting area to give them our pitch." Frowning, Ra-

chel squinted into the darkness. "Just where is Gina?"

Frank shrugged. "She mentioned something about going to the library. She wanted to find a book on automotive repair."

Rachel groaned. "Is she still having car trouble?"

Frank shook his head. "No, she mentioned something about wanting to learn how to cut the brake lines in a BMW."

Lacie stepped forward. "Isn't that the kind of car her husband drives?"

Irma gasped. "Oh, no, she really is going to kill her husband! She'll end up in the slammer for life."

"She's not going to kill him," Rachel reassured them. "Planning different ways to murder him is just Gina's way of working through her pain and anger."

"Well, if you ask me," Kate said, cinching the tie of her trench coat, "the best revenge for getting dumped is success. Make something of yourself and prove to everybody that you're better off without him. That really gets 'em right in the old ego."

Rachel sincerely hoped so. If they were successful in revamping the Miss Valentine pageant, she could watch Drew's ego drop a few notches. The memory of that disastrous dinner still stung. She'd never been more than a means to an end for him. A tool he needed to dismantle the boycott. And when his Cupid strategy backfired, he'd tried to sacrifice himself on the altar of Love. As if she'd have him now!

"Well, we can't wait any longer," Rachel said, checking her watch. "The pageant starts in twenty minutes."

The group disbanded, each person heading for their

designated area. Rachel walked through the backstage door, hoping to find Gina somewhere inside. Technicians and stage hands milled around the wings, barely taking notice of her. She kept one eye out for Drew, the last person she wanted to run into—unless it was with her car.

A tap on her shoulder made her jump. She turned around to see Gina smiling at her.

Rachel breathed a sigh of relief. "Where have you been?"

Gina flipped her dark hair over one shoulder. "Flirting with a security guard. I'm a little rusty, but I still haven't lost my touch."

Rachel rolled her eyes. "You can flirt later, we've got beauty contestants to convert."

"Not a chance, Sister Rachel. According to Red, they're off-limits to commoners like us."

"Who's Red?"

"The two-hundred-and-fifty-pound security guard standing outside the dressing room door. And believe me, he's a pussycat compared to the hellcat pageant coordinator. Her name is Maxine, and she's all claws. Nobody but Miss Valentine wannabes can enter her lair."

Rachel slumped against the wall. "This is just great. Our plan hinges on convincing the women that the Miss Valentine pageant should be more than a girlie show. Now what will we do?"

"We're going undercover."

"Please tell me you're joking."

"It's no joke. Wait until you see the disguise." She pulled two small scraps of red Lycra out of the bag and handed them to Rachel.

"A bikini?" She held it up. "I have freckles bigger than this thing."

"Hey, these bikinis are our ticket into the dressing room. Once we have access to the contestants, we can instigate the mutiny."

"If we don't die of pneumonia first." Rachel dropped the bikini back into the bag. "Why didn't you warn me about this before I went on my Twinkie binge?"

Gina shrugged. "So we've both got a few more bulges than we did ten years ago. It will be good for these young girls to see what happens to a woman's body as she gets older."

"Thanks. That's making me feel so much better," Rachel said, pushing her toward the dressing room door.

BY THE TIME RACHEL HAD wedged herself into the bikini, her mood hadn't improved. Especially when she'd compared herself to the perfect, nubile bodies buzzing around the dressing room. These women bulged in all the right places. Their only worries seemed to be dark roots and tan lines. *Who had tan lines in February?* She was just glad she'd remembered to shave her legs.

"Now I remember why I hate going to the beach," Gina said, tugging up her bikini strap. "Whoever invented Lycra should be shot."

"You look fine," Rachel said, hoping she looked as good as Gina. "We'd better split up and work the room. And watch out for Maxine, she looks suspicious."

They both stole stealthy peeks at the steel-haired

chaperone. She stood by the door, staring at them over her bifocals and making notes on her clipboard.

"That's because we're not performing the proper beauty pageant rituals. We didn't spread Vaseline on our teeth for that perfect smile. We didn't spray glue on our butts to keep the bikini bottom from riding up. And our hair weighs less than the requisite five pounds."

"Gina, I think you've just found the perfect opening. We'll ask the contestants for advice on proper pageant procedure, then make our case for the boycott."

"Sounds good. I'll take the girls at the mascara table and you can start in the curling iron corner."

The first woman Rachel approached wore her bikini like a second skin. She knew from the whispers flying across the dressing room that her name was Valerie and she was the front runner to win the title of Miss Valentine this year.

"Excuse me, Valerie, I was wondering if you could give me some advice," Rachel began, hoping the future Miss Valentine could use her clout to make some changes.

Valerie's smoky gray gaze flicked over her from head to toe. "I think a trench coat would do wonders for you."

Rachel bared her teeth in the form of a smile. Just what she needed, a wise-cracking debutante. "You look like you've been around the pageant circle a few times."

Valerie shrugged. "Enough to know a novice when I see one. You don't stand a chance, honey." She flashed a fake Vaseline smile, then slinked away.

Rachel swallowed a sigh of disappointment, hoping Gina was having better luck. Then she felt a tap on her shoulder. She turned around to see a petite redhead grinning up at her.

"Hi, I'm Mimi Summers. You're new around here."

"I'm Rachel Grant, and I've lived in Love all my life."

"No, I mean you're new on the pageant circuit. I've seen the rest of these gals in various pageants around the state since I was eight years old."

"It almost sounds like an exclusive club."

Mimi flashed another huge smile. "Oh, we're all great friends. All the girls are just great. And I'm sure they'll all want to welcome you here and wish you good luck. I know you'll have a great, great time. All the great friendships I've made here are worth all the time and money and hard work. But it's been great. I hold the record for Miss Congeniality. I've won it five times in the last seven years."

"Wow, that's…great." The woman's exuberant cheerfulness was starting to give her a headache. But at least she seemed open to conversation. Maybe if Rachel could get Mimi in their corner, she could spread the boycott cheer.

"So is the pageant's new hairdresser," Mimi chimed, smiling as she grasped Rachel's elbow and steered her through the crowd of women. "No offense, but you could use some help, honey. Don't worry, José can work miracles. He really is a great guy."

"José?" Rachel echoed in horror. How many hairdressers named José could there be in Love? It had taken her three days to undo the damage the last time he touched her hair. And it still didn't curl the way it used to.

"He works at the television station, but moonlights at all local pageants. Isn't that great? He's a wizard with styling gel. All the girls use him."

No wonder they all had such big hair. She slipped out of Mimi's grasp and ducked out the dressing-room door before José could spot her and inflict permanent damage. Only now she was caught in the narrow hallway, surrounded on all sides by bikini-clad beauties. They moved slowly forward, like a human conveyer belt.

Someone elbowed her in the ribs, another stepped on her bare foot with a spiked heel. Rachel raised herself on her toes, finally spotting Gina among them. She jostled her way over hoping they could find an escape route together.

"This way," Gina called, as loud music filled the hallway.

Rachel cut across the stream of bodies toward the darkened tunnel Gina had entered. She headed toward the light and found herself among another group of beauty contestants.

On center stage.

To her horror, the curtain swept open before she could move. Spotlights illuminated every bulge and flaw revealed by her skimpy bikini. The auditorium was filled with people, but she only saw one of them. Drew Lavery, sitting at the judges table right in front of her, staring at her body in horrified disbelief.

Where was a snowball when you needed one?

The next thing she knew, Drew shot out of his chair

and onto the stage. Several of the women squealed as he barreled down on Rachel.

"I told you she'd get kicked out for being too old," Valerie said in a stage whisper to the woman next to her.

That did it. She'd had it with Valerie and her put-downs. She was thirty years old, not ready for a retirement home. And her body didn't look that bad, even in a bikini. At least her I.Q. was bigger than her bust size. She'd used her body to get on stage, and now she'd use her brains to stay on stage until she accomplished her mission.

Only Drew had other ideas. "Get off the stage."

She tried to ignore the way his gaze kept drifting down her body. "I'm not going anywhere."

"This isn't up for debate, Rachel," he insisted, his voice harsh. "Now get off this stage or I'll carry you off."

She tipped up her chin. "I'd like to see you try!"

She'd never seen a man move so fast. Before she knew it, he tipped her up and over his shoulder. Her head hung at his waist, providing her a perfect view of his backside. And perfect was definitely the word for it.

Blood rushed to her head, and not only from hanging upside down. Drew's strong hands held her firmly by her upper thighs, his fingers brushed against her sensitive bare skin, sending electric tingles throughout her entire body. She shouldn't let him have this effect on her, she told herself firmly. Especially when he was treating her like a lumpy sack of potatoes.

"Put me down," she growled, suddenly aware of the hoots and hollers of the audience. If she thought she looked bad in a bikini before, she didn't even want to think about the view she was presenting them now.

"I will," he snapped, marching toward the exit, "as soon as I get you off this stage." But his path was blocked by television newswoman Candi Conrad, complete with microphone and camera crew.

"Mayor Lavery, may I have a word with you?"

"This really isn't a good time," he muttered.

Rachel raised her head, fighting a wave of dizziness. "It's the perfect time, Candi!"

Candi hurried around to the other side, her cameramen still blocking the escape route. Rachel could only hope they didn't have their cameras pointed toward the bottom half of her bikini. She put that thought out of her mind, and tried to ignore the touch of Drew's hands moving over her bare skin as she struggled to right herself. When his firm grasp on her didn't loosen, she gave up and focused her concentration on the microphone in front of her face.

"Does entering the Miss Valentine pageant put you in an awkward position, Dr. Grant?" Candi asked.

She couldn't be serious. Only if hanging upside down over the mayor's broad shoulder in a skimpy bikini in view of half the town and a television audience could be considered an awkward position.

"I suppose you could say that," Rachel replied wryly. "Or you could say that the mayor of Love is abusing his power. I have every right to be on this stage. Now put me down!"

Drew acceded to her wishes, grasping her bare waist and sliding her slowly down his long, sinewy body. She reached out to him to steady herself when her feet finally hit the ground. It certainly had gotten warm on the stage. Probably from all those bright lights. Drew looked flushed, too, as he shrugged out of his suit coat and draped it over her shoulders.

"You've made your point," he said between clenched teeth. "Now get off the stage. Every guy in the audience can see you."

"Isn't that the purpose of the bikini competition?" she asked, relishing the warmth of his jacket. It smelled like him too, spicy and sexy and so incredibly masculine.

"Rachel, we can debate this later..." Drew began, before Candi honed in between them with her microphone.

"Is this run for Miss Valentine an indication that you're dropping the boycott, Dr. Grant?"

"Of course not," Rachel replied, ignoring Drew's dark glower and clenched jaw. "In fact, this pageant is a perfect example of the way our city's celebration discriminates against a certain segment of the population. Mayor Lavery wants to disqualify me because I don't have a perfect body."

"That's not true," Drew said between clenched teeth, "There's absolutely nothing wrong with her body."

"Then why are you kicking me off the stage?"

"Because I don't happen to like you parading around half-naked in public. Besides, you're just doing this to get back at me."

Her mouth dropped open. "This is not about *us*, Drew."

Candi Conrad stuck her microphone under Drew's

nose. "Is your relationship with the leader of the boycott affecting your job performance, Mayor Lavery?"

"There is no relationship," Rachel insisted, pulling the microphone toward her. "The mayor just wants to deflect attention from the boycott because he knows I'm right. Let's make the Miss Valentine pageant one that celebrates brains as much as beauty. And let's begin by giving out scholarships instead of sexy lingerie as prizes."

"Do you have any comments, Mayor?" Candi asked.

"I agree with everything Dr. Grant says about the beauty pageant. But she's wrong about one thing."

Rachel stood her ground as he moved a step closer to her. "We do have a relationship. She's just too stubborn to admit it."

"There you go," she sputtered, "changing the subject again. We were talking about the Miss Valentine pageant. Now are you prepared to spearhead the changes I mentioned?"

"Yes. Are you prepared to be my valentine?"

The audience gasped. She could see Lacie and Frank in the center aisle with their mouths hanging open in disbelief. Rachel pressed her lips together. He'd trapped her in a corner. Again. Television cameras seemed to bring out the worst in him. "You can't be serious."

"I want you to be my valentine, Rachel. Now are you willing to compromise and meet me halfway?" He took another step closer to her, his blue eyes blazing into hers. "Will you be my valentine?"

Cameras rolled and flashbulbs popped, a hush settling over the audience as everyone awaited her answer. She saw anti-Valentine's Day signs bobbing up and down in the crowd. The members of her support group were out there, depending on her. Looking up to her as their leader. She couldn't let them down.

Just as she couldn't let Drew play any more games with her heart. She took a deep breath and looked him squarely in the eye. "No."

TWO HOURS LATER, Rachel and her group of Valentine's Day protesters sat at a corner table in the Love Nest Bar and Grill, toasting their success. Although Rachel smiled and joked and laughed with the rest of them, all she really wanted to do was cry in her beer. Refusing to be Drew's valentine had been the hardest thing she'd ever done. Even if it was for a good cause.

"We did it," Frank announced, reaching for the basket of popcorn. "Our boycott actually made a difference. I heard they're going to form a special committee to revamp the beauty pageant."

Gina adjusted the tiara on her head. "I still can't believe they voted me Miss Valentine. And without even a drop of silicone in my body! Best of all, my soon-to-be ex-husband was in the audience. Made me glad he was alive just so I could see the expression on his face!"

"Kate was right," Lacie said, sounding surprised. "Success is the best revenge. Where is she, anyway?"

Irma set down her beer bottle, her green eyes sparkling with excitement. "She's getting ready for our trip."

"Trip?" Rachel echoed.

"That's right," Frank affirmed, with a chuckle.

"Kate and Irma talked me into going on a cruise with them. I'm going to try me some deep-sea fishing."

Rachel swallowed. "All three of you?"

"Yep," Frank replied, winking at Irma. "It's a singles cruise for people over fifty. We thought it might be nice to meet some new blood."

In one fell swoop, she'd just lost over half her Transitions support group. "That's...wonderful."

Irma nodded. "I can't live in the past anymore—and my husband would be the first one to tell me so." She clapped her hands together. "I haven't been so excited about anything in years! I'm finally making myself happy instead of waiting for someone else to do it."

"Me, too," Lacie announced. "I'm through waiting around for my boyfriend to come back to me. In fact, I don't want him anymore. I'm going back to college, and I'm going to start a new job teaching ballet to beginners. It doesn't pay as much as my old one, but I can't think of anything that would make me happier."

"Great," Rachel murmured, suddenly realizing her group didn't need her anymore. But what would she do without them?

"We owe it all to you, Dr. Grant," Irma chimed. "This boycott showed us we can do anything if we put our mind to it. And you were just wonderful up there on that stage tonight. I just hope the mayor wasn't too embarrassed when you turned him down on television."

"What choice did I have?" she asked, peeling the beer label off the bottle. "Becoming the mayor's valentine meant betraying the boycott. I couldn't let you all down like that.''

"Let us down?'' Irma echoed, her brow furrowed. ''Dr. Grant, are you telling us that you want to be his valentine?''

"Yes. No. I don't know,'' she said, feeling both foolish and disloyal.

Lacie put down her margarita. ''If you're hot for the mayor, I think you should go for it.''

"That's right,'' Frank said. ''If you don't have to be in love to be happy, what do you have to lose?''

Only her heart. She'd already fallen hard for Drew, but admitting it out loud would make her too vulnerable. There was safety in silence. ''But what if this is all part of his game plan? He just asked the leader of the Valentine boycott to be his valentine. On television! What if it was just a publicity ploy?'' Then she voiced the fear that had been niggling away at her. ''What if he's using me? What if he doesn't really want me after all?''

Gina leaned forward. ''You told me once that love doesn't come with any guarantees. I know you don't want to betray the boycott, but what about betraying your own feelings? Aren't they worth taking the risk?''

A hush settled over the group, broken only when the bartender turned up the volume on the television set.

"This is a special newsbreak from WKLV, Channel five, your local news leader."

"Oh, no,'' Gina cried, grabbing her tiara. ''They picked the wrong Miss Valentine and now I have to give my crown back.''

"This just in," announced WKLV's silver-haired anchorman. *"The votes for Love's Most Romantic Couple contest have been tabulated. The winners are...Mayor Drew Lavery and Dr. Rachel Grant!"*

Everyone turned to stare at Rachel. She fell back in her chair. "That's impossible! We're not even a couple."

"It's true," the anchorman declared. *"You heard it here first. They won by a landslide."* He chuckled. *"It seems everybody in Love has been keeping track of this riotous romance since the sparks began flying between Dr. Grant and Mayor Lavery on WKLV's own morning show, 'A Look at Love.' WKLV sends its congratulations to the happy couple. And now we return to our regularly scheduled program."*

"I don't believe it," Rachel breathed.

"I do," Irma said. "You two kids look good together. If we hadn't been boycotting Valentine's Day, I'd have voted for you myself."

"I did," Lacie admitted, a pink blush on her cheeks. "I know it's against the boycott, but I've always loved the Most Romantic Couple contest. It's so...romantic."

Gina nodded. "Especially the fancy candlelit dinner for two at the ritziest restaurant in town. That's the top prize of the contest. Looks like you'll be dining in style at The Fireside tomorrow night."

"I can't go," Rachel moaned, torn between her loyalty to the group and her desire for Drew. "Tomorrow is Valentine's Day."

Gina stood up. "Everyone in favor of dropping the boycott, raise your hand."

Rachel looked around the table in disbelief as every

hand shot up, their faces wreathed with encouraging smiles. They were all willing to take chances in their own lives, preparing to embark on new adventures. Did she have enough guts to do the same?

"The vote is unanimous," Gina announced, resuming her seat. "The boycott is over, so now you can go." She grinned. "And I recommend the chocolate pecan cheesecake for dessert. It's much tastier than Twinkies."

DREW AWOKE SLOWLY the next morning, his mind still entwined in his dream. He was judging an endless stream of Miss Valentine contestants, and was torn by indecision. He couldn't find the perfect Miss Valentine. Intermixed among the contestants were all his old girlfriends, smiling and waving at him. But he ignored them, focusing on his duty as head judge. He had to pick Miss Valentine. Everyone depended on him.

He watched the contestants stroll across the stage, comparing them all to Rachel. All of them came up short. None of the bikini-clad women had her big brown eyes, her bouncy blond hair, or her long, long legs.

He tossed and turned in bed, starting to panic. Then he saw her. The tall woman standing center stage, holding a snowball...Rachel.

Drew opened his eyes and stifled a groan. His dream had been all too real. Rachel had been on that stage last night. *His Rachel.* Standing under the spotlight in a bikini no bigger than his handkerchief. Revealing every luscious inch of her body. And what a body. Not reed-thin flesh and bones with artificial padding, but a real woman with soft, generous curves. A body that made a man burn. A body that every other man in that auditorium had doubtlessly been drooling over. He probably should have declared a flood watch.

He closed his eyes, trying to block out the memory and fall back into mind-numbing sleep. Instead he began to dream of his favorite breakfast. Crispy fried bacon. Eggs over easy. Homemade cinnamon rolls with sweet white frosting. He sat up in bed, his nose telling him this was no dream. Someone was cooking breakfast. He dressed in record time, then flew down the stairs, hoping it wasn't a mirage brought on by too many frozen pizzas.

"I thought you'd never get up," Kate Lavery said when he walked into his kitchen. She stood at the stove, flipping eggs in a skillet. "It's almost ten o'clock."

Drew rubbed one hand over his unshaven jaw. "I didn't sleep too well."

"You look terrible," his mother said, setting a plate on the table.

"Thanks, Mom." He pulled out a chair, then watched his mother cheerfully flit around his kitchen. "You look…great." It was true. Kate Lavery had a glow about her that he hadn't seen in a very long time.

"I feel great. I'm leaving on a cruise Monday, and I wanted to fix you a bon voyage breakfast."

Drew put down his orange juice. "A cruise? Since when?"

Kate smiled as she sat across from him and picked up a piece of bacon. "Since yesterday. Irma and I were talking about how we'd always wanted to see Greece, then decided what are we waiting for? So we stopped by a travel agency, bought our tickets and are going shopping today for cruise wear.''

"Wait a minute," Drew said, still trying to catch up. "Who's Irma?"

"Irma Dugan, a great gal. She's in my support group."

"What about Frank? I thought you two were an item."

"Frank's going, too. He and I have become good friends, but it's nothing serious. I'm having too much fun to get serious about anyone." She handed him a cinnamon roll. "You know, after your father died, I believed I couldn't make it without a man in my life. I married again too soon, and found out the hard way that I was wrong. I don't want just any man now, I want the right man. Maybe I'll meet him someday, maybe not. In the meantime, I'm planning to have the time of my life."

Drew took a sip of his juice, trying to adjust to his mother's new attitude. "So how long will you be gone?"

"The cruise lasts for a month. Then we thought about checking out Italy." She grabbed her handbag off the table and began digging around inside. "I'll leave you my Detroit Pistons tickets in case you want to catch some games. Maybe you can take Rachel."

He suddenly lost his appetite. "Fat chance. You saw what happened at the auditorium last night."

She reached over to pat his hand. "I know you're not used to women turning you down, Drew, but you have one last chance. Have you heard the big news?

You and Rachel won the Most Romantic Couple contest.''

He nodded. "Charlie called me last night."

"Isn't it exciting?" Kate exclaimed, as she pulled a fifty-dollar bill from her purse. She pushed it across the table to him. "Why don't you make an appointment for a haircut. You want to look nice this evening."

"I don't need a haircut because I'm not going anywhere." He pushed the fifty back across the table. "And I make enough money to pay for my own haircuts. Thanks anyway, Mom."

"You're not going?" Kate looked at him for a long moment. "Drew, don't let your pride get in the way now. You've never given up this easily before."

"She rejected me, Mom. I'm not a glutton for punishment."

"You're not a quitter, either. And neither was your father. I rejected his proposal three times before I said yes. You'll never know how glad I am that he didn't take no for an answer. You've got to give it another shot."

He rubbed his hand across his jaw. "What if she's a no-show? What if she still doesn't want me?"

"You've never backed down from a challenge, Drew. I know you're hurt, but isn't Rachel worth a little extra effort?" She pushed the fifty-dollar bill at him. "Now take the money. I've never reneged on a bet. You won. The boycott is over."

He blinked back his surprise. "Rachel's dropping the boycott?"

She nodded. "That's right. Irma told me they took a vote on it last night. She also told me Rachel is planning to meet you at The Fireside this evening. Now the rest is up to you."

He stared down at the fried eggs congealing on his plate. "I'll have to think about it."

Kate smiled. "Why don't you think about it while you get a haircut?"

A rustling sound startled them both. Drew turned to see Russell leaning against the doorway, still in his flannel pajamas.

"Do I smell real food?" Russell asked.

Drew pocketed the fifty, then made the introductions while Russell padded into the kitchen and helped himself to a cinnamon roll.

"So you're Rachel's ex-fiancé?" Kate asked, with a concerned glance at Drew.

Russell nodded as he licked frosting off his fingertips. "That's right. Drew's been good enough to let me camp out here for a few days, but I'll be leaving tonight. It's time to move on with my life." His gaze leveled on Drew. "Now if I can just find a way to pay him back for everything he's done."

Drew put down his orange juice. "You're finally...I mean, you're leaving? Permanently? As in moving out?"

Russell nodded. "An interim position came up at Michigan State. I'll be teaching there for the rest of the semester. I'm sure you're ready to have this place back all to yourself."

Even better, he could finally have Rachel all to himself. Drew's heart began to race. His mother was right. This was his last chance. No more boycott. No more ulterior motives. No more games. He was still determined to win, only this time the prize was Rachel's heart.

He glanced at the clock on the kitchen wall, realizing how little time he had to prepare for the biggest date of his life. He needed a haircut. And his best suit pressed. Flowers, too. Maybe a huge bouquet of red roses. No, too generic. He wanted to give her a special Valentine's Day gift. As special as Rachel herself.

He hurried through the rest of his breakfast, then left his mom and Russell discussing insects indigenous to the Greek isles. This time he was determined to do everything right to make Rachel Grant his valentine.

BY THE TIME DREW HAD RUN all his errands and driven back to the house, he barely had time to dress and shave before his big date. He set Rachel's Valentine gift carefully on the oak floor in one corner of his bedroom. He grinned at the floppy-eared puppy sleeping soundly in his brand-new doggy bed. It was the cutest mutt he'd ever seen and he knew Rachel would fall in love with it.

He laid newspapers across the floor, then set an ottoman between his dresser and the wall, effectively barricading the sleeping puppy in the corner. That should keep her out of trouble if she awoke.

After dressing with meticulous care, he stood in front of the mirror in the upstairs bathroom, running an electric razor over his stubbly jaw. A splash of cologne and he'd be out the door.

"Hey, Drew, could you come in here a minute?"

Drew clenched his jaw. Russell. He still hadn't

moved out yet. How long did it take to pack a knapsack?

"I don't have a lot of time," Drew said, hurrying toward the guest room. "What do you need?"

Russell stood in front of his bedroom closet. "I just wanted to tell you goodbye." He held out his hand. "Thanks for everything."

Drew reached out to shake hands, then his eyes widened in horror. Russell's entire hand was covered with bright red blood.

His head grew woozy. He reached out to grab the closet doorknob as his knees buckled. From far away he heard the sound of Russell's voice. He sounded amazingly calm for a man bleeding so profusely.

"I know I don't deserve her, Drew. But I won't let my Lovebug get squashed by a heel like you."

Then everything went black.

10

_____

Send me no flowers,
nor candy to eat.
A gift from the heart
just can't be beat.

RACHEL SAT ALONE at the table in the center of The Fireside restaurant, surrounded by television cameras and photographers and news reporters. A huge red banner with the words Most Romantic Couple In Love emblazoned across it hung above the table.

Her mouth hurt from smiling, but she didn't know how else to hide her growing uneasiness. He was late. Only five minutes late, but the patrons in the crowded restaurant were already starting to whisper. She glimpsed Gina and Pam sharing a table in the corner. They were trying very hard not to look worried.

Rachel ordered a glass of wine from the waiter, then sat back in her chair, her gaze riveted on the door. Any moment now, she'd see him walk through it. And he'd have a wonderful excuse for running late. There was a lot of tourist traffic on Valentine's Day. The streets were still a little icy, so he had to drive slow. Maybe he even had car trouble.

Seven-fifteen and still no sign of Drew.

News reporter Candi Conrad got out a cigarette and

moved to the smoking section of the restaurant to flirt with a muscle-bound waiter. One of the cameramen made a call on his cell phone. The violinist hired to serenade the most romantic couple bellied up to the bar.

By seven twenty-five Rachel had memorized the entire menu. She'd give him five more minutes, then order the bottomless bowl of chicken soup so she could drown herself in it. As the seconds slowly ticked by she realized she couldn't even wait that long. Not with everyone staring so pitifully at her. With a fake smile to all the reporters, she pushed back her chair and headed for the ladies' rest room. Gina and Pam followed close on her heels.

"I can't believe he stood you up!" Gina exclaimed after the door closed behind them with a swoosh.

Rachel checked under all the stalls in case a reporter lurked inside, but they were empty. Then she turned on the heel of her Italian suede pumps. "Me, neither. Now what am I going to do? I can't go back out there and pretend nothing is wrong."

Pam held out both hands. "Just stay calm. This is a small crisis. We can handle it."

"It's a disaster," Rachel exclaimed, pacing back and forth. "I've just been stood up in front of the entire town. It will probably be the lead story on the local news tonight. How will I ever live this down?"

Gina shook her head, her mouth pressed into a thin, angry line. "You were right about Drew Lavery all along. The only reason he was romancing you was to stop the boycott. But I can't believe he'd have the nerve to embarrass you in public like this. Talk about poor sportsmanship!''

''And to think I believed him when he asked me to be his valentine last night,'' Rachel said, slumping against the sink. ''He looked so sincere. I actually felt guilty about turning him down. Was that really just another ploy?''

''Face it, Rach, the guy is a rat.'' Gina narrowed her eyes. ''And do you know what we do when we come across a rat?''

''Scream and put the house up for sale?'' Pam ventured.

''No, we exterminate them,'' Gina said. ''Do you remember that movie *Thelma & Louise*?''

''I'm not ready to blow him away. Yet.'' Rachel closed her eyes. ''Even though hurtling off a cliff sounds preferable to facing Candi Conrad and her cotton candy questions. What am I going to do?''

''Stay in here until the restaurant closes?'' Pam suggested. ''I have a deck of cards in my purse.''

Rachel shook her head. ''No, I've got an even better idea.''

''A Twinkie binge?'' Gina guessed.

''No more Twinkies for me.'' Rachel kicked off her shoes. ''I'm going out the window.''

''Rachel, no!'' Pam exclaimed, grabbing her by the arm. ''I won't let you throw your life away. Especially over a jerk like Drew Lavery.''

''Relax, sis,'' Rachel said, ''we're on the first floor this time. I'm only going out the window to avoid all those reporters. I don't want any distractions when I track down Drew. Especially when I tell him exactly what I think of him.''

"Track him down? I'm not sure that's such a good idea," Pam warned. "Why don't you just try to forget about him? He's not worth the effort."

"But I am." Rachel reached up to unlatch the window. "When Russell left me last year, I just let him go. I never tried to find him or contact him. I never demanded any answers. Instead I wallowed in Twinkies for six months trying to figure out why he didn't want me anymore. I'm not going through that again."

"But you were engaged to Russell," Pam countered. "He did owe you answers. Drew is a different story. You two have only gone out on one date."

"Pam's right," Gina said. "Drew never should have humiliated you in public this way, but just think how much more embarrassed you'll be if you go chasing after him."

Rachel considered their arguments. It would be so easy to give up. To go home with some of her pride still intact. But her heart wouldn't let her surrender so easily. Especially since she'd fallen in love with the man.

"Look, I can handle rejection." Rachel looked from Gina to her sister. "But I can't handle not knowing the truth. I need to find out if I ever meant anything to him, or if our date and that kiss, and last night were all part of the game."

Pam looked as if she might cry, and Gina looked even more homicidal than usual.

"Don't worry," Rachel assured them, as she swung one leg over the windowsill. "I'll be fine. Just try to distract all the reporters until I make my get-away.''

She dropped down into a snowdrift on the outside of the building. Shivers coursed through her as Gina passed her shoes through the open window. But they were shivers of anticipation. She couldn't wait until she got her hands on him. Literally speaking. By the time she was through with Mayor Lavery, he'd wish she'd stuck to snowballs.

Rachel waded through the snow until she reached the parking lot, then slung her shoes on her frozen feet. ''Ready or not, Drew. Here I come.''

DREW OPENED HIS EYES, wincing at the bright, bare lightbulb shining above him. He blinked twice, his head still foggy. A faint hint of mothballs mingled with the musty odor invading his nostrils. He sat up on his elbows and looked around. He was in the closet.

It was actually a small dressing room that he'd converted into a walk-in storage closet. The lightbulb illuminated the shelves lining the walls, piled full of boxes. He lay on the dusty wood floor, wondering how he got in here. Then he remembered Russell and all that blood. His head swam again for a moment, then cleared.

He had a date with Rachel.

He swore under his breath as he checked his watch, then lunged for the door. It was locked.

He frowned at it for a moment, trying to make sense of the situation. Why was he locked in the closet? How did he even get in here? And where was

Russell? Drew pounded on the solid oak door with his fist. "Russell, are you out there? The door's locked. I've got to get out of here right now."

"Give it up, Lavery," Russell called from the other side of the door. "It's no use."

"What are you talking about?" Drew shouted. "Open this damn door before I break it down."

"No way. I locked you in there to keep you away from Rachel. So you might as well get comfortable. You're not going anywhere for a while."

Drew gave the door a vicious kick, barely making a dent in the wood but almost breaking his big toe. He hopped around inside the closet, gritting his teeth at the pain. Breaking down the door was not an option. He'd have to use his brains instead.

"Listen, Russ, just open the door and we can talk this out. I know you're upset about losing Rachel…"

"You don't know anything, Lavery," Russell said. "Rachel Grant is the most decent woman I've ever known. And I won't let her be hurt by a user like you."

"Hey, I'm not the one that left her for a dung beetle," Drew shouted, his temper overcoming his good intentions. "Why didn't you just stay lost, Baker, instead of coming back here to stir up trouble?"

"It's a good thing I did come back," Russell countered. "To save Rachel from making the biggest mistake of her life."

"You were the biggest mistake of her life. You hurt her once, and now you're determined to hurt her again. How do you think she'll feel when I don't show up on our date tonight?"

"Relieved," Russell exclaimed, "once I explain the reason."

"You're planning to tell her you kidnapped me? That will be hard to do from a jail cell. Think it over, Baker, you're a smart man. And kidnapping is a crime."

"This isn't kidnapping," Russell said, not sounding at all worried at the prospect of studying insects behind bars. "You fainted in the closet, the door accidentally closed and I'm looking for the key. Don't worry, I should find it in a couple hours."

Drew resisted the urge to kick the door again. A couple of hours? So much for his date with Rachel. He didn't even want to imagine her sitting at the restaurant. Alone. Waiting for him. He closed his eyes and groaned, envisioning the media attention always given to the Most Romantic Couple contest. He could see the headline now: Mayor Comes Out Of The Closet. Would Rachel ever forgive him? What if she didn't believe his story? It was his word against Russell's, and getting kidnapped by an entomologist sounded even more unbelievable than getting lost in the African bush.

"You might as well get comfortable," Russell said. "There's a thermos of coffee in there on the floor and a couple of entertaining entomology texts. You never know when that kind of information will come in handy."

"I don't want to get comfortable," Drew said, fed up with this ridiculous situation. "I want Rachel."

Russell snorted. "Give it up, Lavery. You never wanted Rachel. You just wanted to win your bet."

Drew closed his eyes, dread filling him. "What are you talking about?"

"Don't you remember the wager you made with your mother? Fifty bucks to get Rachel to drop the boycott by Valentine's Day. I was standing outside the kitchen this morning long enough to hear it all."

"You don't understand."

"Oh, I understand perfectly. And I'll wager that the only reason you're so hot to make it to that restaurant is because you've got another bet on the line."

Drew decided at that moment to donate all the money from those ridiculous bets to charity. And he'd kick in an extra hundred to pay for his stupidity. "It was a mistake. I made those bets before I even knew Rachel."

"Bets? Plural? See, I was right. You really are a jerk. And you've been stringing Rachel along for the sake of a few lousy bucks."

This time Drew wanted to kick himself instead of the door. "You don't know anything about me. I happen to love her."

His heartfelt proclamation was greeted with another derisive snort. "Right. Well, we'll just see how she feels about you after I tell her about your little gambling problem."

Drew pounded on the door with both fists. "Just let me out of here and I'll tell her myself."

"So you can put your own spin on it? No way, Lavery. You politicians can make anything sound good."

"You can't keep me away from her forever," Drew countered, looking frantically around the closet for a hairpin so he could try to pick the lock.

"I don't need forever. I'm going over to her place right now to tell her the truth. By the time I'm through she'll never speak to you again."

Drew dug through boxes, throwing old trophies and track medals on the floor around him and tipping over the thermos of coffee. Small drops of coffee seeped through a crack in the lid, soaking into the cover of a book entitled: *The Wonderful World of Insects.*

"She won't take you back, Baker," Drew shouted, "no matter how she feels about me. So if this is some ploy to win her heart, it's going to backfire on you." He heard heavy footsteps on the other side of the door, then the distinct sound of a coat zipper.

"I know it's over between Rachel and me," Russell said, sounding resigned. "We can't ever go back. But I still care about her. And I refuse to let you hurt her."

Drew was running out of options and out of ideas. He couldn't stay cooped up in this closet while Russell set out to ruin his life. "Wait…you can't just leave me in here. I'm…claustrophobic. I'll go nuts."

Russell emitted an unsympathetic chuckle. "You should see a therapist about that problem. I'll ask Rachel if she can recommend one. See ya, Lavery."

Then he was gone.

RACHEL'S HAND HURT from pounding so long on Drew's front door, but she wasn't about to go away. Lights blazed inside the house, so she knew he was hiding somewhere inside. A typical coward. She'd stand out here until she got frostbite if necessary. Finally she heard footsteps, then the front door opened.

Russell blinked at her in surprise. "Rachel?"

"Hello, Russell. Drew really needs to get a doorbell. In fact, I think I'll tell him that in person. Along with a few other things." She stepped inside, stamping the snow off her shoes. "Where is he?"

He swallowed, his Adam's apple bobbing in his throat. "Drew? Well, um, this really isn't a good time."

"Don't tell me you're defending him? You're my ex-fiancé, you're supposed to be on my side."

"I am on your side, Lovebug. I've always been on your side. That's why..." He licked his lips and looked nervously toward the staircase.

Rachel headed in that direction. "He's hiding upstairs, isn't he? He's too chicken to see me."

"Not exactly..." Russell said, heading her off before she could climb up the stairs. "We need to talk."

She heard a rumbling from above, then Drew's frantic voice. "Help! Get me out of here!"

Russell gulped, looking more nervous than she'd ever seen him. He raked his long, thin fingers through his hair. "About Drew..."

"What about him?" Rachel asked, prickles of uneasiness crawling down her spine. "What's going on here, Russell."

He took a deep breath. "Lavery locked himself in a closet and I can't find the key. I've looked everywhere. I was just going out for a locksmith when you arrived. He's getting a little...hysterical."

She pushed past him, taking the steps two at a time. She followed the sound of Drew's hoarse shouts until she reached a big bedroom on the west side of the house. It contained a full-size bed with a white wrought-iron headstand, a maple chest of drawers and a man in the closet.

Rachel moved to the closet door, twisting the brass knob, but it wouldn't budge. "Drew?"

"Rachel!"

The way he said her name made her tingle all the way down to her toes. His voice was full of relief and hope and some other undefinable emotion.

"Rachel, your buggy fiancé is cracking up. He locked me in here."

"Ex-fiancé," Rachel amended, as Russell walked into the bedroom. "And why would he lock you in the closet?"

Russell make a cuckoo motion, circling one finger around his ear. "The guy is delirious. He said he's claustrophobic."

"Drew, are you claustrophobic?" Rachel shouted through the door.

"Of course not!" he exclaimed. "Let's get this straight once and for all. I'm not claustrophobic, I'm not impotent and I'm not making this up. Just look at Russell's hand."

His hand? Rachel looked at Russell. He shrugged and shook his head as he held out his hands for her inspection. They both looked perfectly normal. So did the rest of him. Drew, however, sounded a little irrational.

"Drew, just relax," she called, in her most soothing, professional tone. "Take slow, even breaths and imagine you're in a cocoon."

"I've never been in a cocoon," he replied, sounding more frustrated than ever. "But I have been stuck in this musty old closet for the last hour. That's why I missed our date. Russell is trying to protect you from me."

Russell sighed. "The guy is going wacko. I think he needs a psychiatric evaluation. Should I call the paramedics?"

Rachel jumped as she heard the sound of Drew's fist hitting the door.

"Drop the act, Baker," Drew growled. "We both know you locked me in here. If you're not bleeding all over the carpet, then you must have used fake blood. Once I passed out, you shoved me all the way inside and locked the door."

Rachel looked at Russell. He tugged at his shirt collar and gave her a shaky smile. "What a wild imagination. Why would I do something like that? It's illegal."

"Because," Drew bellowed, "you found out about the bet and thought you needed to protect Rachel from me."

"Bet?" Rachel echoed. "What bet?"

Russell laid a gentle hand on her shoulder. "Maybe you should sit down."

"I don't want to sit down," she said, brushing his hand away. "I want to know about this bet."

"I made a bet with my mother," Drew said, "and with Charlie. Fifty bucks that I'd convince you to drop the boycott by Valentine's Day."

Rachel sank down onto the end of the bed. "So you won."

"I won the bet," Drew agreed, "and I lost my heart. I love you, Rachel. No matter what you think of me now. And if you don't want me in your life, then you'd better make certain I stay locked in this closet. Because I intend to show you just how much I love you just as soon as I get out of here."

Rachel's eyes blurred as she looked up at Russell. "Unlock the door."

He folded his arms across his chest, his jaw set in a stubborn line. "I don't have the key."

"Russell," she said, patient with him, because her heart was full of love, "please open the door."

Russell hesitated. "Do you love him?"

She bit her lip and nodded.

"Hey, Baker," Drew suddenly called out, "is a yellow bug with little red spots all over it considered poisonous?"

Russell perked up. "You don't mean a *Anthrenus scrophulariae,* do you?"

"I'm not sure," Drew replied. "There's one crawling in here on the floor. I'll step on it, then shove it under the door so you can take a look."

"No," Russell shrieked, diving for the door as he pulled a key out of his pocket, "don't touch it." He twisted the key in the lock until it clicked and the door came open. The next moment he lay flat out on the floor, courtesy of Drew's fist.

"You were right, Baker." Drew dropped a thick entomology tome on Russell's chest. "It did come in handy."

Rachel hurried over to her ex-fiancé, who moaned as he sat up on one elbow and gingerly fingered his swollen lip.

"You didn't have to hit him, Drew. Oh, look…he's bleeding!"

Drew averted his eyes. "That's something I'd rather not see," he said, pulling her into the closet and shutting the door behind them. "I've seen enough blood for one day. Besides, I want to remain conscious long enough to tell you how much I love you."

She wrapped her arms around his neck. "I'm waiting."

He circled his arms around her waist, pulling her close as he gazed into her eyes. "I love you, Dr. Rachel Grant, and I want to be your valentine. If you'll have me."

"I will…on one condition," she said, a smile playing on her lips.

He looked wary. "What?"

She stood on her tiptoes to whisper in his ear. He laughed, then hugged her close. "Deal."

"Shall we seal it with a kiss, Mayor Lavery?"

"Definitely," he replied in a husky whisper, then covered her mouth with his own.

He tenderly traced her lips with his tongue. Rachel's lips parted as she melted into him, full of love and pent-up desire. She moaned deep in her throat as his arms tightened around her and his tongue delved into her mouth. Her hands restlessly caressed the length of his back, wanting to draw him even closer. His own broad hands spanned her waist, his fingers flexing as they stroked over her hips.

At last he lifted his head, his breathing as ragged as her own. "Now that's what I call a business transaction. Remind me never to negotiate with you again, Rachel. Because I'll give in to everything just so we can seal the bargain."

She laughed. "Too bad I didn't know that when I first declared the boycott. It would have saved me a lot of trouble. We could have been kissing instead of fighting."

"All that wasted time. We have some catching up to do."

"I'm all yours," she said, slipping one hand in between the buttons of his shirt, relishing the feel of his taut, muscular chest under her fingertips.

He closed his eyes, sucking in his breath, as Rachel continued her exploration. "Don't stop."

A knock on the closet door interrupted their passionate interlude. "Go away, Russell," Drew mumbled, pulling her to him for another kiss.

"This is Candi Conrad from WKLV," trilled a familiar, grating voice. "We're here to interview Love's Most Romantic Couple."

"We?" Drew and Rachel said at the same time, staring in horrified dismay at each other.

"That's right," Candi chimed. "I've got my camera crew with me and we've got a live television remote scheduled in two minutes. There's also a couple of reporters from the newspaper and some other interested people who joined the hunt to track you two lovebirds down."

"Rachel," Gina called through the door, sounding a little frantic. "Are you all right?"

"I'm fine."

"That's an understatement," Drew murmured, his lips lingering on her neck.

"How's Russell?" Rachel asked, pleasantly distracted by Drew's kisses and roaming hands.

"He left," Gina announced. "He grabbed his cockroach case and muttered something about heading back to Africa."

Drew hugged her close. "Just what I wanted for Valentine's Day. Well, besides a picture of you in a bikini. I just hope you like your present just as much."

"My present?" she asked, surprised and intrigued by the sparkle in his deep blue eyes. "Is it flowers? A box of candy?"

"Even better." He grinned. "How do you feel about the patter of little paws?"

Rachel's breath caught in her throat. "Oh, Drew, you got me a dog? A pet of my very own?"

He nodded. "A puppy. She's sound asleep in my bedroom."

"Take me there," she said, her eyes shining with excitement.

"Definitely," he said in a seductive whisper. Then he kissed her again. When they finally emerged from the closet, her cheeks were still flushed from the heat of Drew's embrace.

Everyone started talking at once, with cameras flashing and reporters shouting questions. Candi motioned for silence, then shoved the microphone under his nose and whispered, "We're on the air!"

"I have a short statement," he announced, "and

then Dr. Grant and I have some more negotiating to do. She's agreed to be my valentine." He held up one hand as the crowd burst into spontaneous applause. "And I've agreed to a new town motto, which I'm confident I can pass through the city council."

Rachel's heart beat faster as he grinned down at her, his eyes sparkling with mischief. "Perhaps my opponent would like to tell you Love's new motto."

She stepped forward. "Thank you, Mayor, it would be my pleasure." She smiled, her heart full of love and her life full of dreams. "You Don't Have To Be In Love To Be Happy…But It's A Great Place To Start."

Take 2 bestselling love stories FREE
Plus get a FREE surprise gift!

Special Limited-Time Offer

Mail to Harlequin Reader Service®

3010 Walden Avenue
P.O. Box 1867
Buffalo, N.Y. 14240-1867

YES! Please send me 2 free Harlequin Love & Laughter™ novels and my free surprise gift. Then send me 4 brand-new novels every other month, which I will receive months before they appear in bookstores. Bill me at the low price of $2.90 each plus 25¢ delivery per book and applicable sales tax if any*. That's the complete price, and a saving of over 10% off the cover prices—quite a bargain! I understand that accepting the books and gift places me under no obligation ever to buy any books. I can always return a shipment and cancel at any time. Even if I never buy another book from Harlequin, the 2 free books and the surprise gift are mine to keep forever.

102 HEN CH7N

Name	(PLEASE PRINT)	
Address	Apt. No.	
City	State	Zip

This offer is limited to one order per household and not valid to present Love & Laughter™ subscribers. *Terms and prices are subject to change without notice. Sales tax applicable in N.Y.

ULL-98

LOVE & LAUGH

INTO MARCH!

#63 FROM HERE TO MATERNITY
Right Stork, Wrong Address
Cheryl Anne Porter
Murphy Brown meets June Cleaver? Up-and-coming ad exec Laura Sloan loves her single, child-free life just the way it is. So what's she going to do when she finds an adorable, *abandoned* baby boy in her office *and* her first love, gorgeous Grant Maguire, on her doorstep? Suddenly she's got two males to contend with—and she hasn't a clue what to do with either of them. But Grant's kisses are making her think it's time she found out....

#64 HIS BODYGUARD
Lois Greiman
Nathan Fox doesn't want a bodyguard, but after the last threat on his life he needs one. Luck is on his side when one Brittany O'Shay, petite, curvy and beautiful, applies. He hires her, hoping she'll be more interested in exploring his body than actually guarding it, leaving him free to figure out who wanted to harm him. Little does Nathan know that this is one woman who takes her job seriously... all business and no play. And how he'd like to play....

Chuckles available now:

#61 COURTING CUPID
Charlotte Maclay

#62 SEND ME NO FLOWERS
Kristin Gabriel

LOVE & LAUGHTER™